Best Friends

"I heard about you and the Unicorn Club today," Elizabeth began. "I felt really bad that you didn't tell me about it. But I guess you have a right to do things on your own. I'm trying not to let it bother me."

Jessica jumped up from her bed and threw her arms around Elizabeth. "Oh, Lizzie," she cried. "Thanks for understanding. I wanted to tell you. I just didn't dare. All this pledge stuff is supposed to be a secret. And I haven't even been voted in yet. I'm still scared I'll do something to ruin my chances."

"Don't worry. I know you'll get in." Elizabeth tried to make her voice cheerful, but in the pit of her stomach she felt a terrible emptiness. She was losing Jessica. What was she going to do without her best friend?

SWEET VALLEY TWINS

Best
Friends

Written by
Jamie Suzanne

Created by
FRANCINE PASCAL

A BANTAM SKYLARK BOOK®

TORONTO • NEW YORK • LONDON • SYDNEY • AUCKLAND

RL 4, 008–012

BEST FRIENDS

A Bantam Skylark Book / August 1986
11 printings through March 1987

Skylark Books is a registered trademark of Bantam Books, Inc. Registered
in U.S. Patent and Trademark Office and elsewhere.

Sweet Valley High and Sweet Valley Twins is a trademark of Francine Pascal

Conceived by Francine Pascal

Produced by Cloverdale Press, Inc.
133 Fifth Ave., New York, N.Y. 10003

Cover art by James Mathewuse

ISBN 0-553-15421-4

Published simultaneously in the United States and Canada

PRINTED   IN   THE   UNITED   STATES   OF   AMERICA

O   20 19 18 17 16 15 14 13 12

For Jessica Capshaw

One

"Hey, Lizzie! Wait up!"

Elizabeth Wakefield turned to see her twin sister racing across the lawn in front of Sweet Valley Middle School, her long blond ponytail streaming behind her.

"How come you didn't wait for me?" Jessica asked. "We always walk home together."

"I don't know, Jess. I'm in a hurry." Elizabeth glanced back at the girls Jessica had been talking to. She never had much to say to them. They always acted as if they were stars and all the people around them were the audience. But try and tell that to Jessica.

"Lizzie," asked Jessica, "are you mad at me?"

Elizabeth grinned at her sister. "Me, mad? I mean, what for? You borrowed my barrettes without asking, you made me late for science, you got peanut butter in my hairbrush . . . why should I be mad?"

"But I always do things like that!" Jessica exclaimed.

Elizabeth threw up her hands. "Yes! Exactly!" Then she started to laugh. "It's hard to stay mad at you—it's not any of those things, really. I just get bored around those girls and I have tons of homework, that's all."

"Plus you have to help me with my math," Jessica added.

"Yes, your highness." Elizabeth sighed. It would be a tight squeeze, finishing all her stuff and coaching Jessica too, but she hated to say no to her sister.

The girls started down the tree-lined street toward home.

"Did you see Lois Waller in gym class today?" Jessica asked. "She was practically oozing out of her leotard. Fat everywhere. They shouldn't let a tub like her take ballet."

"Jessica," Elizabeth said, "she can't help it if she's fat."

"She can too," Jessica insisted. "She could lose some weight and she *can* help looking so ugly. I mean, she doesn't have to wear those baggy dresses and let her hair hang in her face."

"*Jessica*," Elizabeth groaned.

"Well, she was ruining our class," complained Jessica. "Ballet is supposed to be beautiful and graceful, and she was crashing around like a rhinoceros. It's tough on the kids with real talent."

"Like Ms. Jessica Wakefield?" Elizabeth teased.

"Absolutely. I know I'm better than the other kids. Maybe I'll be a famous ballerina someday. I'm going to practice a whole lot."

"Jessica," Elizabeth said suddenly, "I have great news!"

"Don't tell me we're finally getting our own phone!"

Elizabeth laughed. "Even better. Mr. Bowman is going to let us start a newspaper just for the sixth grade. I asked him today. And he put *me* in charge! You could write a gossip column or something!"

"Caroline Pearce would be better at that. She knows every drop of gossip practically before it happens. She even knows about the seventh and eighth graders."

"How about fashion, or TV?"

Jessica just looked bored and shook her head no.

"You mean—you don't want to write for it?" Elizabeth was shocked. She and Jessica always did things together. They dressed alike, they shared a room, they watched the same programs on TV, they went shopping together. They were best friends.

"I just don't think I'll have time, that's all," Jessica said casually.

Elizabeth tried not to feel disappointed. But it

would feel awfully strange to do something so important without Jessica involved. "Well, I think the paper will be great," she said, " but I know you're busy."

"Okay, big sister."

Elizabeth smiled. It was one of their favorite jokes. She was only four minutes older than Jessica, but that still made her the big sister. Besides, she was the one in charge. She had to remind Jessica to do practically everything, plus help her with her math, and pick up after her. Where would Jessica be without her?

The girls reached their corner, turned down the driveway to their big split-level house, and let themselves in through the kitchen door. Usually they were the first ones home. Both their parents had jobs. Their mother worked part-time at Sweet Valley Design and their father headed a busy law practice. Their older brother, Steven, was a freshman at Sweet Valley High. Sometimes he stayed after school for basketball practice. But just at that moment he came in, slamming the kitchen door behind him and throwing his knapsack on the floor.

"What's wrong with you?" asked Jessica as Steven rummaged angrily through the refrigerator.

"None of your business," he snapped.

Elizabeth and Jessica rolled their eyes. Practically from the first day Steven started high school, he'd been a royal pain.

The twins sat down at the kitchen table with a package of Oreo cookies while Steven slumped down in a chair with a giant slice of cake.

"Cute outfits," he said, smirking, as he looked from one sister to the other.

"What's the matter with them?" Elizabeth wanted to know.

"Nothing," Steven said, "if you like having double vision. Don't you think you're a little old to be dressing the same?"

"No," Jessica said.

"No wonder nobody can tell you apart."

"They can too!" Jessica said. But Elizabeth kept quiet. Kids at school were always staring at her and saying, "Uh . . . Jessica?" Elizabeth looked across the table at Jessica. It was like looking into a mirror. She saw her own blond hair pulled back into a ponytail, her blue-green eyes and long lashes, and even the dimple in her left cheek. She also saw the same white blouse and red sweater-vest, and she knew that under the table were the denim skirt and white knee socks and running shoes she was wearing. But so what? Dressing alike was part of the fun of being twins.

"It would take a detective to know which one of you was which," mumbled Steven, his mouth full of cake.

"Okay, okay, we get the point," said Elizabeth. "But we like dressing alike. We're the only identical twins at Sweet Valley Middle School."

Steven started to say something else, but the phone rang and he and Jessica both dashed for it, knocking over their chairs. Jessica got there first.

"Hello?" Elizabeth could hear her say breathlessly. "Oh, hi." Jessica cradled the phone against her ear and walked into the dining room, stretching the cord as far as it would go.

"That was Lila Fowler," Jessica announced, strolling back into the kitchen. She sounded as though she'd been talking to a member of the royal family.

"Who cares?" Steven said. Then he got up and sauntered out of the kitchen.

Elizabeth knew all about Lila Fowler. She had the biggest wardrobe in Sweet Valley. Her father was rich and bought her everything she wanted. Jessica had been spending a lot of time with her lately, although Elizabeth couldn't understand why.

"She's in the Unicorn Club," Jessica told her sister.

"What's that?" Elizabeth asked. "Did Lila's father buy her a unicorn?"

"This is nothing to joke about," Jessica declared in a superior tone. "It's called the Unicorn Club because unicorns are beautiful and special and everyone likes them. Just like the girls in the club. Hardly any sixth graders get to join. But Lila's in, and Ellen Riteman, too. They're so lucky. Of course, Janet Howell is Lila's cousin."

"And who's Janet Howell?" Elizabeth asked.

Jessica sighed. "Don't you know anything? Janet Howell is only the prettiest, most important girl in eighth grade. She's the president of the club."

Elizabeth leaned forward. "Listen, if you're really so up on everything," she said seriously, "you ought to write for the newspaper."

"No!" Jessica said. "And please don't ask me again, Lizzie."

"Sorry." Elizabeth changed the subject. "Let's go start our homework. Okay?"

"You go ahead," Jessica told her. "I want to practice ballet." Her blue-green eyes began to sparkle. "Especially those curtsies ballerinas make at the end when everyone applauds and throws flowers." Jessica darted out of the kitchen, leaving a trail of Oreo crumbs across the table.

Typical Jessica, Elizabeth thought. Elizabeth got a sponge and quickly wiped the table. Then she headed upstairs to her bedroom, dropped her books on her bed, and flopped down after them. She gazed around the room. It was pretty, Elizabeth thought, but maybe a little babyish. The wallpaper was white with pink flowers, the rug was pink, and she and Jessica each had a white spread and pink pillows on their beds. Pink and white, pink and white. Elizabeth didn't even like pink very much. It was Jessica who chose it. And Jessica's side of the room was an unbelievable mess. Sweaters, tissues, socks, chewing gum wrappers, jewelry—junk was spilling out everywhere. Elizabeth wasn't sure how her twin would be able to unearth her bed that night.

With a sigh Elizabeth settled down at her desk and launched into her homework. She kept on going until just before dinnertime, when her mother called her down to set the table.

Jessica had to be ordered up from the basement to help make the salad. She kept complaining that ballet was a lot more important than food, and then disappeared again. She came to dinner still dressed in her leotard.

"What's this?" Mr. Wakefield asked.

"Oh, Daddy," exclaimed Jessica, "we're taking ballet in gym and I just adore it. I'm the best one. Liz is almost as good," she added hastily.

"Maybe you girls would like to take ballet at the Dance Studio, too," Mrs. Wakefield suggested.

"That would be nice, Mom," Elizabeth said calmly, while Jessica leaped from her seat.

"Are you serious?" Jessica shrieked.

Mrs. Wakefield laughed. "Of course I am. I'll call the studio first thing tomorrow."

Over dessert Elizabeth told her parents and Steven about getting permission to start a newspaper. "And you know what? It will be the first sixth-grade newspaper ever," she finished.

"Oh, honey, we're really proud of you," her mother said.

"Tomorrow I'm going to ask Amy Sutton and Julie Porter to be on it," Elizabeth exclaimed. "I can't wait."

Jessica made a face. "All you need is Winston Egbert and you can call it the 'Nerdpaper,'" she said. "I mean, honestly. Amy Sutton does her homework at *recess* and she wears such boring clothes and Julie—"

"Jessica! You are really unbelievable! Amy and Julie are a lot smarter and more interesting than the snobby girls you think are so great. And what gives you the right to say that—you don't even want to be *on* the paper!" Elizabeth exclaimed.

There was a surprised silence.

"I am much too busy," Jessica said in her most haughty voice.

"Well, Tweedledum and Tweedledee actually have separate interests," Steven said, smirking. "Or anyway, one of them does."

"I have plenty of things on my mind, too," Jessica declared. "You'll see."

Elizabeth had a feeling Jessica was telling the truth. There *was* something on her mind. And it had nothing whatsoever to do with her twin sister. Somehow, for no good reason, that really bothered her.

Elizabeth climbed into bed that night feeling very tired, but she couldn't fall asleep. She still couldn't believe that Jessica would rather spend time with snobby, boring girls like Lila Fowler. Well, she could only hope that Jessica would change her mind. After all, they were twins. And no matter what Steven or anybody else said, twins belonged together.

Two

◇

The next morning Elizabeth decided she wouldn't say a single word to Jessica about the newspaper. She'd just talk to Amy and Julie and get it started. Then, when the paper turned out to be really great, Jessica would be thrilled to be in on it.

Jessica seemed to be in just as much of a hurry to get to school as Elizabeth was. After a quick breakfast the twins picked up identical blue book bags and dashed out the kitchen door. "Let's take the shortcut past the Mercandy house," Elizabeth said. "Maybe I'll be able to catch Julie and Amy before class."

By the time they reached school, the grounds were already crawling with kids. Sweet Valley Middle School was much bigger than elementary school. It sprawled out in every direction on acres of lush green lawn. The twins loved it there, although finding a friend before homeroom was a definite challenge.

"Hi, blondie!" a voice suddenly called.

Both girls spun around.

Bruce Patman was strolling past them with a big grin on his face. He was a really cute seventh grader from one of the richest families in town. Unfortunately, he thought he was the most important person in the world, and he often acted like a bully and a jerk, at least in Elizabeth's opinion.

This was a perfect example. Bruce thought it was hilarious to call them both "blondie." He said it was much easier than trying to tell them apart. Some of the other kids had even started doing it too. Elizabeth could just imagine what Steven would say if he ever found out.

"I wish he'd stop that," Elizabeth muttered, then she noticed that Jessica was paying no attention. She was smiling and staring dreamily after Bruce as though he were a rock star or something.

"Elizabeth," she whispered, "I think Bruce likes me! Mom says boys only tease the girls they like."

Elizabeth was dumbfounded. "I thought you hated boys!" she exclaimed. "All summer long you kept saying how gross they were."

"That was ages ago," Jessica said airily. Suddenly she started jumping up and down and waving. "There they are," she cried. Lila Fowler and

Ellen Riteman were sitting on the school steps waving back. "I've got to talk to them," she told Elizabeth, and darted across the lawn.

Elizabeth took two steps after Jessica and stopped in her tracks. She had almost forgotten the newspaper! It was very easy to get swept along by Jessica Wakefield. But not this time. She had other things on her mind. Elizabeth hurried off to find Julie and Amy.

She felt as though she had covered every inch of the school, when suddenly she saw them—just as the homeroom bell started to ring. "Oh," Elizabeth cried, "I've got something exciting to tell you! And there's no time."

Amy's eyes lit up. "Let's meet for lunch," she said.

Elizabeth hesitated. She and Jessica usually sat together in the cafeteria. But, she decided, Amy and Julie could join them. With a little luck, Jessica might decide she liked them.

At lunchtime Elizabeth and Jessica dashed to the cafeteria and grabbed their usual table. They were just about to sit down, when they both gasped, "Oh, I forgot!" They looked at each other.

"Lila and Ellen asked me to sit with them today," Jessica explained. "I guess you could come along if you really wanted to, but . . ." Her voice trailed off.

"I wanted to talk to Amy and Julie anyway," Elizabeth said quickly. "See you," she called as she watched her blond twin disappear through the crowded cafeteria. It was weird, Elizabeth thought. She would a million times rather talk to Amy and Julie than sit with those other girls, but she still felt as though she were losing out on something.

"Elizabeth! Here you are," Julie said breathlessly. Amy was at her side. "We stood in that lunch line forever."

"What did you want to tell us?" Amy asked as they sat down.

Suddenly Elizabeth felt nervous. Suppose Amy and Julie thought her idea was a big yawn, too? She took a deep breath. "I was thinking it would be fun to start a sixth-grade newspaper. It's okay with Mr. Bowman. I thought we could have interviews and stories about class events—"

Julie's eyes were sparkling. "I just love advice columns and inquiring reporters who go around asking kids stuff like 'What do you think about going steady?'"

Amy interrupted. "And a gossip column; that's a must. And sports, and movie reviews, and a poetry corner—am I getting carried away?"

"I guess you like the idea." Elizabeth laughed. "Let's start writing stuff down."

All three girls opened their notebooks and were scribbling away when Caroline Pearce suddenly plunked herself down next to Elizabeth.

Elizabeth groaned inwardly. Caroline Pearce lived two doors away from the Wakefields and was the prissiest person in the world. Caroline also had the biggest mouth in Sweet Valley. Telling her a secret was like posting it up on a billboard.

"Guess what?" Caroline said, looking very smug. She glanced at the girls' notebooks and they snapped them shut. "They're going to fire Nydick."

"Mr. Nydick? *Now?* At the beginning of the year?" asked Amy.

Mr. Nydick, the head of the history department, was the oldest teacher in the school, and one of the nicest.

Elizabeth was shocked. "How come?"

"I don't know," replied Caroline. "But he must have done something horrendous, maybe to one of the kids. Do you know what else? Roberta Manning was grounded for a week for staying out really late with a *high school* boy."

"Caroline," Elizabeth demanded, "how do you know what the eighth graders are doing?"

Caroline looked mysterious. "I hear things," she said. She stood up. "See you."

"Gosh," Julie said breathlessly, "a high school boy."

"Yeah," Elizabeth said. Even if Caroline's stories weren't always a hundred percent accurate, she couldn't wait to tell Jessica.

On the other side of the cafeteria Jessica was sitting with Ellen, Lila, Janet Howell and three seventh graders, Kimberly Haver, Betsy Gordon, and Mary Giaccio. Jessica had never been more excited in her life. She felt as though an enormous spotlight were shining on the table. Kids kept looking their way, and she had lost count of the cute boys who had waved hello. She could hardly blame them. Every girl at the table was sensational-looking and dressed in great clothes. Jessica knew she could hold her own in the looks department. With her silky blond hair, blue-green eyes, and perfect features, there was no doubt about it. But the other girls at the table had one thing in common that she didn't share—they were all members of the Unicorn Club.

More than anything in the world, Jessica wanted to belong to the Unicorn Club. And she was more determined than ever to find a way in.

"So . . . what do you do at your meetings?" Jessica asked.

"Well," Lila drawled, tossing her long light-brown hair behind her shoulders, "I guess we can tell you." She leaned across the table and lowered her voice. "A lot of times we talk about people, like who's going out with who and who's breaking up with who."

"Oh," said Jessica, feeling slightly disappointed.

Ellen took over. "And," she whispered dramatically, her blue eyes flashing, "we talk about boys."

Jessica straightened up. "Oh," she said with a knowing smile.

"The thing is," Janet went on, "we're always a group. We sit together at lunch. We hang out together after school. Lots of times we go to the Dairi Burger."

The Dairi Burger! That was where the high school kids hung out. Jessica had never been there without her parents. This was getting better and better.

"We plan things, too," Janet added. "Like, this year we decided purple is our favorite color, so we all bought purple stuff to wear."

Jessica checked the girls' clothes. They *were* wearing an awful lot of purple.

"We pay dues every week," Lila said, "to cover expenses—like food for slumber parties. This Friday we're going to Guido's Pizza. We've got enough money for four large pizzas with everything."

"*Four?*" repeated Jessica. They must be big eaters.

"There are twelve of us in the club," Ellen said. "And some boys might drop by our table."

"We don't want the club to get any bigger," Janet put in. "It's exclusive."

Jessica felt her hopes begin to fade.

"But," Lila said meaningfully, "a few new Unicorns—like Ellen and me—get in every year to replace the kids who graduate or move away."

Jessica held her breath. "Is there room for anyone else?" she managed to ask.

"Maybe," replied Janet, looking straight at her. That was all Jessica needed to hear. When Jessica Wakefield wanted something, there was no "maybe." There was only "yes."

Three

◇

The next morning Elizabeth woke up with a start. A horrible groan was coming from her sister's bed.

"Jessica!" she whispered. "What is it?"

"Ohhh," Jessica moaned. "I didn't finish half my homework. All that rotten math. Lizzie, I've just got to copy yours."

"Jessica, Ms. Wyler would kill us if she found out. And I don't want to get in any trouble. I'll help you with the problems during homeroom, okay?"

Jessica made a face. "All right, Miss Perfect." She struggled out of bed and stood in front of the closet. "You know," she told Elizabeth, "we don't own nearly enough purple. Why don't we have more purple clothes?"

Elizabeth shrugged. "Because we don't want to look like grapes?"

Jessica giggled. She finally picked out jeans, a white turtleneck, and her lavender sweater.

Elizabeth quickly pulled on the same outfit.

"Lizzie," Jessica asked a minute later, "I can't find my sneakers. Have you seen them?"

Elizabeth shook her head.

"Can I borrow yours, then?"

Elizabeth was just sliding her feet into her new sneakers. "I've worn my sneakers only twice," she explained. "And they look so good with my jeans. Can't you wear something else? How about your docksiders?"

"Elizabeth, no one wears docksiders anymore. Please let me borrow your sneakers. Just this once?"

"Oh, all right." Elizabeth sighed. "Try to keep them clean though. And while we're on the subject, why don't we clean out this place after school?" She nodded toward Jessica's side of the room. "Bruce Patman could be under that mess and you wouldn't know it."

"I wish." Jessica giggled. "Okay, let's. And thanks. Boy, what would I do without you?"

"I don't know," Elizabeth said seriously.

On the way to school Elizabeth suddenly remembered Caroline Pearce and her stories. "Hey," she exclaimed, "you know what Caroline told me yesterday? They're going to fire Mr. Nydick."

"You're kidding me! He's been around forever."

"No, honest. You know what else? Roberta Manning was grounded for staying out late with a *high school* boy!"

"I know," Jessica said disdainfully. "She got kicked out of the Unicorn Club for that."

"For that?" Elizabeth was amazed. "I bet half the girls in the club are dying to go out with a high school boy!"

"That was probably just the last straw," Jessica said as though she were telling a major secret. "She and Janet weren't getting along very well. Besides, I heard this boy kept putting the Unicorns down."

Elizabeth didn't answer. No matter what they talked about lately, the conversation always seemed to get around to the Unicorns. Jessica seemed to think it was the world's most fascinating topic. But if Elizabeth heard one more word about them, she was going to scream. They were about five minutes from school. Only one other thing might hold Jessica's attention that long. She switched the subject to ballet.

That did the trick. Jessica chattered away about how much she loved to dance and how good she was, right up and into homeroom.

After classes Elizabeth went to her usual spot on the lawn to wait for Jessica. She was actually looking forward to cleaning the bedroom when they got home, even if the mess wasn't hers. The room wouldn't look like a junkyard for a change, plus she'd have the whole afternoon with Jessica.

But where was she? The school grounds were emptying out. Jessica was usually late, but this was ridiculous. Finally, the truth hit her. Jessica was not going to show up. She had been waiting for almost a half hour. And Jessica hadn't even cared enough to let her know she wasn't coming. She didn't know who made her feel worse—herself, for waiting forever like a wimp, or Jessica, for having no consideration at all. Elizabeth picked up her book bag and headed for home.

Jessica, meanwhile, was strolling with Lila Fowler toward the Dairi Burger. She had seen Lila after the last class of the day, and Lila had invited her to have a milk shake with some of the Unicorns. As soon as Jessica heard that, she had forgotten everything else, including her sister. When they reached the Dairi Burger, Lila led her to a table where Kimberly Haver and Ellen Riteman were sitting with Janet Howell. As soon as they saw her, the girls looked at one another and grinned as though they knew a huge secret. Jessica's heart began to pound.

Even before their order came, Janet said in a serious tone, "Jessica, we wanted to meet you here for a very important reason."

Jessica's heart increased its pace. "Yes?" she said breathlessly.

"We have room for two more girls in the Unicorn Club," Janet went on. "We ask only very special people, you know, girls who can keep up the image of the club. And—" She paused dramatically. "We think you're Unicorn material."

Jessica's heart was really racing now.

"Do you know about the pledge tasks?" Janet asked.

"Pledge tasks?" Jessica asked.

"They're our initiation. After we see how you do your pledge tasks, we vote on whether to let you into the club."

Jessica sat up a little straighter. "What do you want me to do?"

"Well," said Lila, "you have three tasks. First you have to hide Mrs. Arnette's lesson plan book at the beginning of social studies and get it back into her bag by the end of class—without her seeing you."

"The Hairnet's lesson plan book?" Jessica gasped. "She can't do anything without that. It's practically glued to her hands." Mrs. Arnette had been at the school almost as long as Mr. Nydick, and every day—without fail—she carefully arranged her hair in a net. Her lesson plan book was like her security blanket. Jessica thought of something else. "Hey," she squealed, "she never lets anybody out of their seats!"

"That's right!" Lila grinned at Jessica. "Second, you have to stand outside the girls' room between classes and tell at least three girls that the bathroom floor is flooded so they're supposed to use the boys' room. And you actually have to get three girls to go into the boys' room."

"Oh, no!" shrieked Jessica.

"And last, you have to come to school one day looking so different from Elizabeth that no one would know you're twins."

"How am I going to do that? Plastic surgery?"

"We didn't say it would be easy," Lila answered. "Now, remember, the pledge tasks are top secret. You can't tell anyone why you're doing them. Not a soul. And that includes your sister."

Jessica thought of something. "So Elizabeth can't tell me her tasks either—"

"Elizabeth?" Janet looked dumbfounded. "What do you mean?"

"Well, you said two new members. She's going to be the other one, isn't she?"

"The other new member," Janet said, "is Tamara Chase, that eight grader who just moved here. We weren't planning to ask Elizabeth. She's nice and all. But she's not right for the Unicorns."

Jessica felt shocked. She wanted to stick up for her sister, but what could she say? She and Elizabeth *were* different, very different. It was hard to see Elizabeth fitting in with the Unicorns. Janet definitely had a point.

The only problem was Elizabeth. She might not see it that way at all. Jessica really didn't want to hurt her sister's feelings, but there was no way she would turn down the chance to join the most fantastic club in school. She'd been dreaming of it ever since she first heard of the Unicorns.

Well, thought Jessica, she had promised to do

her pledge tasks without Elizabeth finding out. Suppose she just didn't say anything at all about the Unicorn Club—not even that she had been asked to join? Then she could still become a member, and Elizabeth's feelings wouldn't be hurt—or, at least, not right away. Later, when she was in, Jessica would probably think of a way to tell her and fix everything.

That's it, Jessica thought. *I'll just keep the whole thing a secret.*

But it wasn't going to be easy. Not at all. How was she going to keep her own twin sister from finding out the best thing that had ever happened to her?

Four

◇

"Jessica, where were you today?" Elizabeth demanded as soon as her sister set foot in the house.

Jessica clapped her hand over her mouth. "Oh, I forgot! I was with the—with Lila Fowler," she said quickly. "I ran into her after school and she asked me to go for a snack." This was all true.

"I waited for you for ages. Don't you remember? We were going to clean our room—meaning your half. You could have told me."

"I know. I'm truly sorry. It just popped out of my head. Look"—Jessica was in a hurry to change the subject—"I bought us these purple belts today." She pulled a package from her book bag. "We can wear them tomorrow. See?" She held the belts up. "We'll look terrific."

Elizabeth felt her anger fade away. Jessica hadn't really forgotten her completely—although she had forgotten she didn't like purple. "That was nice of you, Jess. I guess you can't help being a scatterbrain. Although," she couldn't help adding, "you could try to remember these things."

"Next time I'll tie a million strings around my fingers, promise. Hey, did you finish cleaning the room?"

Elizabeth could not believe her sister. "Are you kidding?"

"I just thought, since you weren't doing anything anyway . . . I know it's my mess, but it doesn't bother *me*. . . ."

Elizabeth started to giggle. Maybe that was how Jessica always got around her. She was so outrageous, it was funny.

"I did not touch one candy wrapper," Elizabeth said. "But I'll clean up with you now."

"Great! But first we've just got to see how the belts look with our white shirts, and there's a good movie on . . ."

As they went up the stairs, Elizabeth thought to herself, *We won't get much done, but we'll have a good time. Things are getting back to normal again.*

Jessica woke up the next morning with butterflies in her stomach. Today was the day. She had to tackle pledge task number one—Mrs. Arnette's lesson plan book. It was going to be hard enough to steal it away from her in the first place, but to have to get it back into her bag, and all during the same class . . . wow! And what if Mrs. Arnette caught her? The Hairnet might be wimpy, but she got tough over anything that even hinted of dishonesty. A "breach of trust" she called it. Jessica could just see herself being dragged to the principal with Mrs. Arnette screaming, "Expel the thief!"

But this kind of thinking would get her nowhere. *I will not get caught,* she said to herself. *I will get the lesson plan book. I will be a Unicorn!*

When she got to school, Lila and Ellen were waiting for her. "Are you ready?" Lila asked.

"As ready as I'll ever be. I've got a plan."

"Oh, I can't wait!" cried Lila. She was in Jessica's social studies class.

"Good," replied Jessica, "because I'm going to need you."

"Wait, Lila can't help you with a pledge task," said Ellen. "Pledge tasks have to be done on your own."

"It's just one teeny-weeny thing. I need Lila to create just *one* little distraction. I'll do everything else all by myself."

"What sort of distraction do you want?"

"Could you get the Hairnet talking?" Jessica asked. "Just ask her something about World War Two. You know how she is on that subject."

"Doesn't everybody?" Lila grinned. "Okay."

By the time the girls got to social studies, Mrs. Arnette was already in the classroom, hairnet firmly in place, the lesson plan book wedged in her arms. Jessica grimaced and glanced at Lila.

She had prayed that the book would at least be lying on the teacher's desk.

When most of the students were seated, Mrs. Arnette flipped her book open. "Are there any questions about last night's homework?" she asked the class.

Jessica nodded to Lila. This was it.

Lila's hand shot up.

"Yes, Lila?"

"I was wondering if you could tell us again about when you were a wacko in World War Two."

"A Wac," Mrs. Arnette corrected her. She patted her hairnet. "Why, yes, Lila. The Wacs were the Women's Army Corps, of course, and my experiences are relevant to . . ." She set the plan book on her desk and walked over to Lila. Jessica breathed a sigh of relief.

"Let's see," Mrs. Arnette continued, deep in thought.

Jessica raised her hand and waved it frantically. "May I leave the room?"

"I'm sure you can wait, dear. A little control, you know. We Wacs learned that on the front lines." Mrs. Arnette didn't want anyone to miss a single second of her class.

Jessica tried to look embarrassed. "It's an emergency," she said with a little tear in her voice.

Mrs. Arnette waved her out and focused on Lila again.

Jessica made a dash for the door, counted out two minutes, and slid back into the classroom.

Mrs. Arnette was still talking away. As Jessica passed the teacher's desk, she casually picked up the book and held it behind her back as she made her way to her seat. A few snickers came from the back of the classroom.

Mrs. Arnette never stopped talking. Each time it seemed there wasn't a single thing left to say about World War II, someone would come up with one more question. The only problem was that most of the time Mrs. Arnette was looking right at Jessica—and somehow Jessica had to get the book into Mrs. Arnette's bag. The bell was going to ring in five minutes.

Mrs. Arnette finished a point and returned to her desk. Her right hand reached absently for her lesson plan book.

Jessica's stomach tied itself into a knot.

Mrs. Arnette looked through the papers on her desk. "Dear me," she said. "Where's my . . .?"

Jessica and Lila stared at each other.

"Class, has anybody seen my lesson plan book?" Mrs. Arnette asked.

Nobody said a word.

There were three minutes left until the bell rang.

"Mrs. Arnette?" Across the room a hand waved wildly. It belonged to Winston Egbert, usually one of the quieter kids.

"Yes, Winston?"

"I don't know where your book is," he said. His eyes strayed to Jessica. "But can you show us how the Wacs stood at attention, you know, eyes forward like during a drill?"

Mrs. Arnette's frown disappeared. She stiffened up, marched across the room, saluted Winston, and stared ahead. When Mrs. Arnette's back was turned, Jessica rose from her seat. She tiptoed up and crouched down behind the big desk. Mrs. Arnette's ancient briefcase was on the floor. Jessica began to fumble with the clasp. She could hear Winston saying, "And what did your uniform look like?" The bag suddenly opened with a snap like a rifle shot. At the same time the bell rang and Jessica shoved the book in. She stood up.

"And on our heads," Mrs. Arnette was saying as she caught sight of Jessica. "My, you're in a hurry today, dear. Let's not forget your homework." Then it all came back to her. "My lesson book . . . I'm sorry, children. No homework tonight."

A loud cheer went up as everyone hurried out. Mrs. Arnette was still sifting papers, muttering, "I could swear . . ." Winston was in front of Jessica.

"Not bad, Winston," she called, and watched his ears turn tomato-red.

As soon as she was in the hallway, Jessica turned to Lila. "Phew!" she exclaimed. "I did it!"

"And," Lila added, "you got us out of a night's homework, too!"

*   *   *

Jessica waited until Friday to tackle her second pledge task. She didn't dare ask Lila to help her on this one. She'd simply have to stake out the girls' room and hope she'd get lucky. She figured the second-floor bathroom was her best bet. Not many eighth graders used it. They'd be hardest to trick.

As soon as the bell rang after third period, Jessica stationed herself on the second floor and put on a no-nonsense expression. Ellen and Janet were standing across the hall from the girls' room so they wouldn't miss anything.

The hallway was already swarming with kids, and right away two eighth graders headed for the girls' room door.

Jessica stepped in front of them. "Sorry," she said. "The girls' room is flooded. No one's allowed in."

"Who're you?" demanded one of the girls.

"The bathroom monitor," Jessica said crisply. "You're supposed to use the boys' room across the hall. Just until the workmen finish."

The girls looked at each other. "Come on," said the other one, shrugging. "We'll go to the first floor."

The first floor! Jessica's heart sank. She hadn't thought about the other girls' room. What if everyone remembered it? She'd be lost.

The eighth graders were three feet away when Lois Waller stepped up.

"You can't go in there." Jessica barred the

way. "It's an absolute lake. The Hairnet told me to keep everybody out while the workmen fix the leak."

"Well, what am I supposed to do?" Lois puffed.

"Use the boys' room." Jessica pointed across the hall.

Lois looked doubtful.

"There are only two and a half minutes left before fourth period," Jessica warned her. She was counting the seconds.

Lois's face fell. "Okay."

Jessica watched nervously as Lois crossed the hall and hesitated under the sign that said BOYS. Cautiously she pushed the door open, poked her head in, and listened. Then she went inside, the door swinging shut behind her.

She was out in one second. "There are *boys* in there," she announced indignantly, and fled down the hall.

"That has to count," Jessica called to Janet. "She went all the way in."

Janet was laughing so hard she couldn't answer, so Jessica knew she had scored.

One down, two to go.

Jessica was feeling pretty smug until she saw who was headed for the bathroom next—Amy, Julie, and Elizabeth. Jessica nearly fell over. Now what should she do? There was no way she was going to embarrass her own twin. Jessica decided to let Elizabeth speak first.

"Hi, Jessica!" said Elizabeth. "What are you doing?"

"Oh, waiting for Lila," Jessica said quickly.

"Come on, Elizabeth," Amy said. "The bell's going to ring."

"See you later." Elizabeth disappeared into the girls' room.

Jessica watched glumly. Out of the corner of her eye she saw Janet shaking her head. What if she thought Jessica wasn't fit to be a Unicorn?

But Jessica didn't have time to worry. Two more girls were coming her way. Eighth graders by the looks of them. Too bad. They were her only chance.

"Sorry," Jessica said in a firm voice. "Bathroom's flooded. You'll have to use the boys' room."

The taller girl looked suspicious. "I just saw someone go in."

The seconds were ticking away. Jessica groped for an answer. "Oh, sure. . . she's in the Future Plumbers Club."

"Future *Plumbers*?"

"They're not very active, but they're great in emergencies. Anyway, I'm the bathroom monitor and I'm supposed to send you to the boys' room."

The second girl started to laugh. "Come on, Janie," she said. "I've always wanted to see inside a boys' room!"

A smile spread across Janie's face. "Let's go!"

Jessica held her breath. As soon as the door to

the boys' room closed behind the girls, she heard screams and shouts. She didn't wait a second longer. She and Janet and Ellen took off down the hall, laughing like crazy.

Jessica decided to wait until Monday to try her last pledge task. This was the very worst one. Looking different from her identical twin would be hard enough, but doing it without telling Elizabeth seemed nearly impossible. Still, there had to be a way. She started to think. Elizabeth always put on the same outfit her sister did. But maybe this time, Jessica thought, she could arrange things so that Elizabeth had to get dressed first. And maybe, she thought, the ideas coming faster now, she could borrow some of their mom's stuff and make herself look older than Elizabeth.

On Monday morning, according to plan, Jessica stayed in bed while her sister stood in front of the closet. "What should we wear today?" Elizabeth asked.

Jessica yawned. "You got me." She rolled over and pretended to doze off.

"Come on, Jess. Make up your mind," Elizabeth said.

Jessica kept her eyes closed and her breathing even.

Elizabeth looked at her twin. "OK," she said. "The yellow sweat suits."

Through her lashes Jessica saw Elizabeth lay out both outfits, dress quickly, and start downstairs. "Pancakes, Jess," she called over her shoulder.

In two minutes Jessica was out of bed and in an entirely different outfit. Then she grabbed her mother's hot curlers and stood in front of the bathroom mirror. She rolled the ends of her hair lightly around the fattest rollers. After a few minutes she gently brushed out a mass of curls. Next she touched some mascara to her eyelashes and carefully put on lip gloss. The change was amazing. She looked like a different person—much older and very glamorous.

Jessica checked the time. She and Elizabeth would have to leave for school in less than ten minutes. Perfect—as long as Elizabeth didn't make a fuss.

Jessica took a deep breath and ran downstairs. When she walked into the kitchen, conversation stopped dead. Her parents, Steven, and Elizabeth just stared at her.

Then her mother's face broke into a grin. "Sweetheart, you look so different!"

"You look so grown-up." Her father was smiling.

"Not bad," commented Steven, which was about as close to a compliment as he ever came, at least these days.

"You do look different," Elizabeth said quietly. It was clear she was upset and trying not to show it.

"I just used Mom's curlers," Jessica said with

relief in her voice. She figured she was lucky Elizabeth was still speaking to her. And it looked like she was going to keep quiet.

"Maybe I'll try it!" Elizabeth cried. She pushed her chair back and stood up.

Uh-oh, Jessica thought.

Mrs. Wakefield put her hand on Elizabeth's arm. "There isn't enough time, honey."

"I forgot. We'd better go," Elizabeth said. She gathered her books and started for the door.

Jessica threw down her napkin and ran after her sister. "Lizzie, wait for me!"

Elizabeth stopped and waited, but she didn't say a word. Jessica kept up a steady flow of small talk as they walked along, even though her sister was barely listening.

They were almost at school when Elizabeth finally said, "Jess, why didn't you tell me you were going to do this?"

"Do what?" Jessica wore her most innocent expression.

"Please don't start, Jess. Why did you change the way you look?"

Jessica was squirming inside. Then she had an inspiration. "I just decided Steven was right. We're too old to dress alike."

"But you could have warned me. We've been dressing alike since nursery school. Why didn't you tell me?"

"It's really no big deal. It was time for a change, that's all." Jessica had noticed Bruce Patman. Just wait until he saw the new Jessica Wake-field.

Bruce caught sight of the twins. "Hey, bl—" he started to say, and then, "Heyyy." He whistled after them.

Elizabeth flashed a disgusted look at her sister, but Jessica was in a different world, blushing and smiling at Bruce.

"Jess, couldn't we—"

Before Elizabeth could say another word, Lila and Ellen ran up. "Jessica, you look gorgeous!" exclaimed Lila. The girls began talking excitedly. Elizabeth slipped away.

As soon as she was gone, Lila lowered her voice and said, "Janet saw you walking to school. She says to tell you that you did a good job on all your pledge tasks. We'll vote on you by the end of the week."

"The end of the week!" Jessica moaned. "That's practically forever! I don't know how I'll stand it!" But deep down she wasn't worried at all. She knew she would get what she wanted. Jessica Wakefield was definitely going to be the next member of the Unicorn Club.

Five

◇

In the girls' room on the first floor Elizabeth locked herself in one of the stalls and began to cry. She just didn't understand. It felt as though Jessica were moving on and leaving her behind. All of a sudden she was going places without asking her along, and doing things without telling her about them. And now Jessica looked so different from her that no one could tell they were twins.

She heard the girls' room door swing open, and choked back a sob. It was two sixth graders she didn't know very well.

"I've just got to do something with my hair," one was saying. "Did you see Jessica Wakefield? She must have had a makeover. She looks so much older. She doesn't even look like her sister anymore. It's amazing. I mean, now you know who's who."

"That's a relief," the second girl said. "I wanted to get to know them better, but I was always afraid I'd start using the wrong name or something."

The door slammed and Elizabeth was alone again. But now she knew exactly what she wanted to do. She stood in front of the mirror. She undid her ponytail and let her hair fall free. Then she parted it in the middle, pulled it back from her face, and fastened it with a clip. It was a hairstyle she loved and Jessica hated. She studied her reflection. She looked good, really good. Like a new Elizabeth Wakefield.

After a last look she left, just as Lois Waller was coming in. "Hey, Liz!" Lois's eyes were wide. "You should wear your hair like that all the time."

Elizabeth smiled. "Maybe I will," she said.

And all day long, all over school, she heard the same thing. She looked great, Jessica looked great, and it was absolutely great that they had started wearing different clothes.

There was only one no vote. Mrs. Arnette sighed. "How sad it is that you and your sister aren't dressing alike! You used to look like two little dolls," she said.

We probably did, Elizabeth thought. *Ugh*.

At dinner that night the family admired her new look too.

"Now I have two sophisticated daughters," her father said.

"It's funny," Elizabeth said. "I thought I

would hate it, but I like looking different from Jess. I guess we won't be dressing alike anymore."

"Hallelujah," Steven muttered, while Jessica gasped, "Never, ever?"

Elizabeth had to smile. "Maybe once in a while," she said.

"Oh, good." Jessica was relieved. "I still love us being twins. It's fun to dress alike."

"Oh, girls," Mrs. Wakefield suddenly exclaimed. "I've got good news. I called the Dance Studio and a beginners' ballet class is just starting. Tomorrow, in fact. It meets twice a week."

"Ballet," Steven snorted. "Big deal."

But Jessica let out a shriek. "Oh, Mom! Thanks!"

Elizabeth was happy, too. Looking different from Jessica was one thing, but spending time away from each other would be something else entirely. She still wanted to be with her twin as much as she could. Now they could practice together—just as Elizabeth had hoped they would.

The next afternoon, the twins walked to the Dance Studio together. "I've been practicing so hard," Jessica exclaimed as she hurried Elizabeth along. "And look"—she held her dance bag open and pointed inside—"a new leotard."

Elizabeth pulled it out. "Purple! What about your black one?"

"Black is so boring," Jessica said. "I borrowed purple leg warmers from Lila. Maybe I'll dye my slippers, too. I really want to stand out."

"Mom will kill you if you dye your shoes!"

"Not if you don't tell her," Jessica said, and changed the subject. "Guess what? I caught Bruce Patman looking at me today. I really think he likes me."

"I don't know what you see in him. He's a jerk and he's always picking on people. He calls Lois 'the pig.' The other day in the cafeteria he stood up and shouted out everything Lois had on her lunch tray. All the kids were laughing at her."

"Well, it must have been pretty funny," Jessica said. "She gets enough food to feed an army."

"But, Jessica," Elizabeth said, "that doesn't give Bruce the right to make fun of her in front of everybody."

They had reached the Dance Studio. As they pushed open the heavy glass doors, Jessica whispered, "I'm so excited! I just know it's going to be wonderful!"

The receptionist was sitting at a large, overflowing desk just inside the entrance. She smiled as soon as she saw them. "Now, don't tell me. You're the Wakefield twins. I'm Mrs. Hanley."

She pulled out a clipboard and checked off their names. "Go hurry and change and then go on into the studio. Most of the other girls are already inside. Madame André will be right with you." She waved toward the door.

Jessica squeezed her sister's hand. "Madame André! She's the head of the whole studio. Are we lucky!"

The dressing room was empty. "We'd better get moving," Elizabeth said, aware that Jessica's window-shopping along the way had made them late.

Quickly she slipped into her black leotard, white tights, and black slippers. Pretty standard, she thought as she watched Jessica pull her colorful leotard from her tote bag.

Jessica was looking into the mirror and patting her hair, now back in its old ponytail. She had a little smile on her face. "I wonder . . ." she murmured. She noticed Elizabeth in the mirror behind her. "Oh, Lizzie, you go ahead. It'll take me another minute to get ready. I want to look just right for Madame André."

"OK, slowpoke." Elizabeth smiled. "But hurry up. Class is going to start any second."

"I'll be right there." Jessica waved her away.

Elizabeth went into the studio. It was a huge room, with mirrors lining two walls and the barre running along a third. About thirteen other girls were waiting for Madame André. Elizabeth recognized just one of them—Sarah Thomas from her math class. They smiled at each other.

"Attention!" A stern voice with a French accent boomed through the studio.

Elizabeth whirled around. A tall woman with gray hair pulled back tightly into a bun was striding toward them. She held her head very high and she did not smile.

"I am Madame André," she went on crisply.

"Today we begin the study of ballet. I will demand hard work from you, but you will enjoy the dance." Madame André held a long stick in her hand and she rapped the floor with it to emphasize her words.

Elizabeth looked nervously toward the door to the dressing room. What on earth was keeping Jessica? Elizabeth was sure Madame André expected all her students to be on time. And Jessica really wanted to impress her.

"Class, please face the front and sit on the floor while I call the roll. *Alors*, we begin." Madame André rapidly called out names from an alphabetical list in her hand, studying each face as the student raised her hand. Finally, she reached the W's. Jessica still hadn't appeared.

"Elizabeth Wakefield?" she called. Elizabeth raised her hand. She was so nervous for Jessica, she thought she would faint.

"Jessica Wakefield?"

"Here! I'm here!" Jessica appeared at the door to the studio. Now Elizabeth was positive she was going to faint. She couldn't believe her eyes.

Jessica was wearing the purple leotard and Lila's purple leg warmers, which were purple with pink hearts and yellow stripes. Besides that, she had knotted a filmy lavender scarf around her waist, and she had untied her hair so that it tumbled over her shoulders in waves. The sides were pinned with glittery barrettes. Long lavender streamers dangled from the barrettes. Last, but definitely not least, she had smeared blue eye shadow all the way up to her eyebrows.

"Mademoiselle Wakefield!" barked the teacher.

"Yes?" Jessica said timidly.

"What is this costume? Did you think we were performing? First lesson, and you are a star? In the ballet class we are simple. The dress is plain. *Comprenez-vous?* Do you understand? No purple. No—none of *this*." She crossed the room to Jessica, untied the scarf from her waist, and tossed it onto the piano bench. "We wear the hair back, out of the face. It must not get in the way of the dance."

Elizabeth felt terrible. Poor Jessica! She was just trying to look exotic and graceful. But Madame André was staring at her as though she were a monster.

Jessica's face had turned white. It was true. Every other girl in the room was wearing her hair in a braid or a bun or a ponytail.

Madame André handed Jessica a rubber band. "Take off those things and fix your hair so you look like your sister." She looked toward Elizabeth and nodded as though she were relieved that one Wakefield was a proper ballet student.

Her hands trembling, Jessica unfastened the barrettes and pulled her hair into a ponytail.

"And next class," the teacher continued, "be here before roll is called, like the others. And no purple. Pink or black or white—like your sister, *non*? And no makeup! Here we have no stars, only hard workers!"

Jessica nodded. She looked as if she wanted to cry.

As soon as Madame André turned her back, Elizabeth squeezed Jessica's hand. "Don't worry," she whispered. "It'll be OK."

But it wasn't.

Jessica was too upset to concentrate. She did everything wrong during the class. First she mixed up the five positions, which Elizabeth knew she could do perfectly. Then she lost her balance holding a plié and tripped.

"*Très bien*, Elizabeth! Very good, Sarah!" Madame André kept saying. Or sometimes, "Back straight, Mademoiselle Thomas. Feet out!" But she didn't say a word to Jessica—not even when she tripped. She just looked at her coldly and called out, "*Très bien*, Suzanne!" to the littlest girl in the group.

When the hour was over and Madame André finally dismissed the class, Jessica turned to Elizabeth with her eyes full of tears. "I really messed up," she said. "I ruined everything." They walked to the dressing room together. "I can do all that stuff. Better than anyone else. She just got me so nervous."

"I know." Elizabeth put her arm around her sister. "You'll do better next class. Madame André will forget all about today."

Jessica sniffled. "I hope so." But she was beginning to wish she had never come to the Dance Studio. She had a feeling ballet was going to be one huge mistake.

Six

◇

"Elizabeth, why didn't you tell me?" Caroline Pearce galloped across the cafeteria and practically tackled Elizabeth.

"Tell you what?" Elizabeth was totally puzzled.

"About your sister."

Elizabeth gave Caroline a blank look.

"And the Unicorns! Jess is so lucky! Hardly anyone gets asked to join the Unicorns."

Join the Unicorns! Elizabeth's stomach did a flip-flop.

Caroline rattled on. "I heard she did a great job on her pledge tasks. It's just too bad they didn't have room for you, too." Caroline's eyes were glued to Elizabeth's face.

Elizabeth wasn't listening anymore. "Yeah," she said. "Look, I'm sorry. I've got to go now."

She walked out of the cafeteria as fast as she could.

She felt as though someone had knocked the wind out of her. Jessica joining the Unicorns! This had to be the biggest thing in Jessica's life. And she hadn't told her about it—not a single word. Elizabeth's eyes filled with tears. Jessica would spend every free minute with the Unicorns now. And Elizabeth would be on the outside.

Suddenly she remembered that she and Jessica were supposed to walk to ballet together right after school. For the first time in her life Elizabeth didn't want to be alone with her sister. Not now. Not the way she was feeling. She searched the halls frantically for someone who had a class with Jessica. There was Lois Waller—they had math together. "Lois," she called, "could you tell Jess I can't walk to ballet with her today?" Lois looked thrilled at the chance to do the favor.

"Sure!" she called back.

Somehow Elizabeth dragged herself through the afternoon. She dreaded the thought of facing Jessica. She just couldn't stand to ask her about the Unicorns, but somehow she had to. When she reached the Dance Studio, Jessica was already there.

"Here I am," Jessica said cheerfully. "Ms. Punctuality!" Then she looked at her sister. "Anything wrong?"

Elizabeth just shrugged and said, "Not really."

"You look funny. You sure you're all right?"
Elizabeth nodded.

Jessica decided this wasn't the time to worry about anything except ballet. She just had to make up for Tuesday's lesson and impress Madame André. She wore a plain black leotard like Elizabeth's and had pulled her hair into a tight ponytail. She thought she looked totally boring, but if that's what Madame André wanted, that was what Jessica Wakefield would give her.

Jessica made sure she was the first one in the studio, and when Madame André strode in with her roll book and pointer, Jessica sat down before anyone else. She had positioned herself right in front, so the teacher would see how perfect she looked. She waited for Madame André to mention the change or at least nod or something to show she noticed. But when she called Jessica's name, Madame André looked right through her.

The entire hour was the same. It was all *"Bon,* Elizabeth!" and *"Très bien,* Elizabeth!" but for Jessica, nothing at all. By the end of class Jessica felt absolutely invisible.

"Boy!" she said to Elizabeth in the dressing room. "I just can't believe this! And after all the trouble I went to. Wait until I tell the Unicorns—"

Elizabeth burst into tears.

"Lizzie, what's wrong?" Jessica cried.

"Oh, Jessica!" Elizabeth choked as she grabbed her clothes and ran out of the Dance Studio.

Jessica stared after her. Suddenly she had the worst feeling. She just knew that Elizabeth had found out about the Unicorn Club. *But it wasn't my fault*, Jessica told herself. *I had to keep everything secret. And after all, I didn't try to upset Lizzie. It just happened.*

"Mom, can I talk to you?" Elizabeth asked Mrs. Wakefield as soon as her mother got home.

Mrs. Wakefield was just hanging up her jacket and putting her briefcase away. She turned and saw her daughter's tearstained face. "Oh, baby," she said. "What happened?"

Elizabeth just shook her head. She couldn't speak.

"Let's go into the den," her mother suggested. She closed the door behind them.

"Now," she said, "can you tell me what's wrong?"

"Jessica's going to be a Unicorn," Elizabeth burst out, "and she kept it secret. She doesn't tell me anything. We never do things together anymore. And she doesn't even care!" Elizabeth began to sob.

"Calm down," her mother said soothingly. "Let's go back to the beginning. You said Jessica is a *unicorn*?"

Elizabeth took a deep breath. "There's this club at school," she explained. "The Unicorn Club. It's only for the girls who are pretty and popular.

It's a really big deal. Only a few sixth graders get asked to join."

"Is it something you'd like? What does the club do?" her mother asked.

"I don't know," Elizabeth sniffled. "Talk about boys, I think. Boys and clothes. Anyway, they didn't ask me."

"But honey," her mother said, "that doesn't sound like something you'd enjoy. It sounds right for Jessica, but not for you."

Elizabeth wiped her eyes. "I guess I don't know if I'd want to be in it, but I still sort of wish they wanted me. Maybe it's really not the club. It's just that we used to do everything together, and now Jessica doesn't even want me around."

"I know that's not true," Mrs. Wakefield said. "But twins can't be together all the time. It's good for you to do different things."

"Really?" exclaimed Elizabeth. "Jess and I should be apart?"

"Yes," her mother said gently. She hugged her daughter. "You're growing up, that's all. And there's not a soul in the world who hasn't hit at least one rough spot growing up. Just remember— your father and I are here to help. You'll see. You'll find more and more things to do on your own."

"I guess so." Elizabeth sighed, but she still felt miserable. Her mother really didn't understand. She needed to spend *more* time with Jessica, not less. How could she let the Unicorn Club break them up?

Elizabeth found Jessica up in their room. She was sprawled on the bed polishing her nails. "We'd better talk, Jess," she said.

"Okay," Jessica said nervously. She was almost sure she knew what Elizabeth wanted to talk about.

"I heard about you and the Unicorn Club today," Elizabeth began. "I felt really bad that you didn't tell me about it. But I guess you have a right to do things on your own. I'm trying not to let it bother me."

Jessica jumped up from her bed and threw her arms around Elizabeth. "Oh, Lizzie," she cried. "Thanks for understanding. What did Mom say?"

"She said it's good that we have separate interests."

"Oh, good. Lizzie, I'm sorry. I wanted to tell you. I just didn't dare. All this pledge stuff is supposed to be secret. And I haven't even been voted in yet. I'm still scared I'll do something to ruin my chances."

"Don't worry. I know you'll get in." Elizabeth tried to make her voice cheerful, but in the pit of her stomach she felt a terrible emptiness. She was losing Jessica. What was she going to do without her best friend?

Seven

◇

The next morning Jessica woke up even before the alarm went off. She was much too excited to sleep. It was probably the most important day of her life. She rolled over and saw her sister lying in bed, her eyes wide open. "Lizzie!" she said. "This is the day! The Unicorns are voting on me!"

"I know," Elizabeth said. She had a funny look in her eyes.

"What were you thinking about?"

Elizabeth smiled. "The old days. Remember the time we made a camp for Barbie and Ken out front, and this real tough kid came by and said he was going to wreck it, but you talked him into playing Barbie with us?"

Jessica giggled. "Then his big brother came along and called him a sissy, and he started pulling Ken's and Barbie's arms off. Then they ran off with Ken." She stopped. "Did they give him back?"

"I think they got sent to reform school. Ken's probably sharing their cell." Elizabeth sighed suddenly. "I kind of miss stuff like that."

"Not me," Jessica said. "But I like to remember it."

"Maybe that's what I meant. But I am going to miss you."

"Am I going somewhere?"

"Well, sort of. Once you're in the Unicorn Club, we'll hardly see each other. Mom says we should do things separately, but I think it will be horrible."

"Hey!" cried Jessica. "I've got a great idea. If I get into the club, I'll get you in, too."

"Could you really? Then things could stay the same!"

"Sure," Jessica said. She knew the Unicorns thought Elizabeth wasn't right for the club, and she could see what they meant. But there had to be a way to get her in. Maybe it wouldn't be easy, but that had never stopped Jessica Wakefield. She propped herself up on her elbows.

Just then the phone rang. Jessica made a mad dash for the extension in the hall. She came back into the room a moment later looking shocked, and closed the door.

"You will never in a million years guess who that was!"

"Who?"

"It was Roberta Manning—for *Steven*. Steven must be the boy Roberta's in trouble over! I told her Steven was still sleeping." She smiled slyly.

"Hey, I wonder when Steven's going to get up." Jessica's face was full of mischief.

"Why?"

"Why? I want to talk to him about Roberta Manning. For once we could get some gossip before Caroline."

"But Jessica, he'll have a fit. And he's your own brother. Do you really want the whole school gossiping about Steven and Roberta? Don't forget, she was a Unicorn. That's not going to be great for your image. The Unicorns sure won't like it—they just want people to know how popular they are, how gorgeous they are, and how perfect. Besides, didn't you say Roberta's boyfriend made fun of the Unicorns?"

Jessica clapped her hand over her mouth. "Oh, my gosh!" she cried. "I didn't think of that! Promise you won't say a single thing about it to anyone!" She acted as though Elizabeth had been planning to broadcast the news.

Elizabeth crossed her heart. "Not one word."

That afternoon Jessica threw open the kitchen door and shrieked, "I made it! I made it! I'm a Unicorn!"

Elizabeth forgot all her feelings about the

club. She leaped up from her seat at the kitchen table and gave Jessica a big hug.

"Oh, Jess! I'm so happy for you!" she cried.

"What's going on?" Steven came through the door.

"Steven!" exclaimed Jessica. "I'm a Unicorn! They voted on me this afternoon."

"A Unicorn in the family. Aren't we lucky. So when do you get your horn?" Steven tossed his knapsack on the floor and walked out of the room.

Jessica looked at Elizabeth. "Things must be rotten with Roberta."

"Let's just leave him—" Elizabeth stopped speaking when she saw Steven standing in the doorway.

"Just what was that crack?" The twins had never seen him so mad.

"Oh, nothing," Jessica said, backing away.

"You better remember this, both of you. Stay out of my business. I don't want to hear that name in this house." Then he was gone.

Elizabeth and Jessica stared at each other.

"Whew! What was that all about?" Jessica said.

"You got me, but I wouldn't mention Ro—her anymore. Let's forget about it. This is a happy day for you."

"It sure is!"

"Jess," Elizabeth asked, "how soon do you think you can try and get me into the club?"

Jessica had forgotten all about that. "I don't know," she said vaguely. "After a while."

Elizabeth seemed to wilt. She gave a big sigh.

Jessica had a load of math homework that night and she wanted Elizabeth in a good mood.

"I just mean not in my *first* meeting," she said quickly. "But I can probably do it in my second!"

Elizabeth brightened right up. That wasn't long at all.

On Monday afternoon Jessica went to her first official meeting of the Unicorn Club. Elizabeth decided not to mope around. She invited Amy Sutton over. They had a lot to talk about anyway, and there never seemed to be time enough in school.

Elizabeth put her things on the kitchen table. "Do you want a snack? I like peanut butter and banana sandwiches, but don't be embarrassed if you think they're gross. Jessica gags when she looks at one."

"I can understand that." Amy was starting to giggle. "But then, I like peanut butter and pickles."

"Jess would have you arrested." Elizabeth laughed.

"I don't tell many people," Amy said.

"Let's eat outside," Elizabeth suggested. "There's this great place where I go all the time. It's under an old pine tree."

"Hey, neat!" Amy exclaimed when she saw it.

Elizabeth parted the branches. "It was our hideout when we were little. See, we made a bed of pine needles over here. This big root is the couch, and the branch that dips down is like a chair. This is where I write stories sometimes." She paused. "Jess never comes here anymore. She thinks it's babyish, I guess."

"Well, I don't. It's nice and private. We could have meetings about the newspaper here. Top secret."

"Which reminds me," Elizabeth said. "We still have to come up with a name for the paper."

Amy groaned. "All my ideas are so blah—*The Sweet Valley News*, for instance."

"I know what you mean. What do you think of *The Chatterbox*? It's Julie's idea."

Both girls shook their heads. "Nooooo," they both said, then they were quiet.

"Well, it should have 'Sweet Valley' in it," Amy said.

"And something about the sixth grade," Elizabeth added. *"The Sweet Valley,"* she said slowly—and then it came to her. *"Sixers!"*

Amy looked amazed. "I love it. It's perfect."

"I didn't have any ideas before," Elizabeth said.

"You sure do now! There's just something about working with someone else, I guess." Suddenly Amy's eyes lit up. "Why don't we try to write a book? I read about a kid our age who did it."

"A whole long book? About what?"

"Us. The kids at school. Real stuff."

Elizabeth was beginning to feel excited. "That would be wonderful. I haven't been doing much of anything, except the newspaper. And ballet."

Amy frowned. "My mother keeps trying to get me to take ballet. She hopes it will make me graceful and ladylike."

"*My* mother wants me to be more independent."

"Why can't our mothers just let us grow up by ourselves?" asked Amy. "We're not stupid. We could do it. Hey, can I ask you something? How do you feel about Jess being in the Unicorns and not you?"

"Mostly—mixed up. I didn't even like those girls before, but now—it's just that the club will take up all Jess's time. What do you think of the Unicorns?"

"They are sort of . . . glamorous. But most of them have as much personality as a hairbrush. All they can think about is what clothes to wear or who's going to win the football game." She looked at her watch. "Hey, it's late! The time went so fast. I'd better go."

After Amy left, Elizabeth thought about the afternoon they had spent. It had really been great. It was too bad, though. Once Jessica got her into the Unicorns, she worried that she wouldn't have time for her other friends anymore. But it would be worth it, wouldn't it?

Eight

◇

It was perfect. Jessica was at her third meeting of the Unicorn Club. She was actually sitting on Janet Howell's white canopy bed. Lila and Ellen and all the other Unicorns were trying out different hairstyles and talking about Jessica's favorite topics—where to get the greatest clothes and how to get the cutest boys.

There was only one problem. Somehow Jessica had to figure out a way to get Elizabeth into the club—even though the Unicorns didn't really want her. Elizabeth was just not going to leave her alone until she kept her promise.

Finally, Jessica decided to come right out with it. At the first pause in the conversation she clasped her hands together and said, "I have a suggestion, everybody."

"What is it?" Janet asked.

"I think the Unicorns should take on one new member. She's really pretty and very smart—"

"Who is she?" asked Janet.

"Elizabeth Wakefield," Jessica said simply. She tried to look as though she expected everyone to start cheering.

"Your *sister*!" Janet exploded. "Jessica, we talked about that already. We said Elizabeth wasn't right for us."

"Since I've become a member I've changed my mind," Jessica said as brightly as she could. "I think she'd be perfect."

"What a baby," snapped one of the eighth graders. "Can't you do anything without your sister? Come on, you're a big girl now."

It was time for a different approach. "Oh," Jessica said sadly. "Then I—I'll have to drop out of the club."

"*What?*" cried six girls all at once. "Why?"

Jessica made her voice waver slightly. "It's just that . . . well, my parents . . . they think that twins . . ." Slowly, Jessica began gathering her things together.

"Wait a second," Janet said. She called a conference in the hallway with the two eldest members of the club. Two minutes later they were back.

"Look, Jessica, we don't want you to drop out. I mean, how would it look? It's OK for us to kick people out, but it's different for somebody to quit. So—we're going to give Elizabeth one pledge task, and it's not going to be an easy one."

"I'm sure she would do anything. Will you really give her a chance?" Jessica asked.

"Sure," Janet said. "Ask her to sit with us at lunch and we'll tell her what the task is."

"Great!" Jessica exclaimed. "That's all my parents can ask for—a chance." To herself she added, *Jessica, you are a genius!*

As soon as Jessica got home, she told her sister the good news.

Elizabeth looked as if she had just gotten the best present in the world. "Oh, Jessica," she cried. "This is wonderful! Now we can be together again!"

The very next day Jessica led Elizabeth to the Unicorns' special table in the cafeteria.

Janet got right down to business. "OK, Elizabeth," she began, "Jess probably told you we're thinking of letting you join the Unicorns. But before you get in, you have to do a pledge task. If we like the way you handle it, we vote on you."

Elizabeth nodded.

"Of course, we're going to make it easy on you. Most girls get three tasks. We're giving you only one."

"That's fine with me," Elizabeth said.

"Here's what you have to do," Janet went on. "Invite Lois Waller to go to the Dairi Burger with you after school on Wednesday. Order two ice cream sundaes, and when they're ready, say you'll get them while Lois saves your table."

Elizabeth kept nodding. This didn't sound bad at all.

"Then, on your way back, scrape the whipped cream off Lois's sundae and cover it with this instead." Janet reached into a bag on the table and pulled out a can of shaving cream. "Can't you see her face when she gets a mouthful of this glop?"

"Make Lois eat shaving cream?" Elizabeth cried. "No way! I can't do that to someone. Especially not to Lois. Everyone's already so mean to her." Elizabeth stood up.

Jessica gasped. "Elizabeth!"

"Look, think it over." Janet didn't look surprised at all. "It's your ticket into the club. Take it or leave it. Just let us know tomorrow."

Elizabeth left the table.

Behind her Jessica faced the rest of the girls. She was furious at her sister. "She'll do it," she said. "Believe me, she'll do it."

Elizabeth slumped down in a seat next to Amy and Julie.

"Wow," Amy whispered, awestruck. "They want you to join, don't they?"

"Yes," Elizabeth said angrily. She wadded her lunch bag into a tight ball. She would never play such a rotten trick on Lois, or anyone else. Not in a million years.

*   *   *

The minute Jessica got home she marched straight to the pine tree in the backyard. She was sure Elizabeth would be out there.

"How could you do that to me?" she cried. "You made me look like a fool. Do you know how hard it was to—to—Oh, Lizzie, you can't say no!"

"Jessica, I'm sorry. I really want to be in the club with you, but I won't do that to Lois."

"You are a priss. A first-class priss!"

"You can call me whatever you want," Elizabeth said in a firm voice, "but there are some things I won't do, and hurting a kid like Lois is one of them."

"You're not going to poison her," Jessica objected. "She's just going to taste it."

"That's not what I meant. It would embarrass her."

Jessica rolled her eyes. "It's only a joke. It'll be funny. Everyone will laugh."

"*At* Lois. Jessica, I can't do it." Elizabeth turned her back. "That's the end of it."

"That's what you think!" Jessica snapped. Then she whirled and stalked into the house. There was no way Elizabeth was going to make a fool out of her. In another minute she was talking on the phone to Janet Howell.

"OK," she said, her voice low. "Elizabeth changed her mind. She'll do it. And Wednesday will be fine." Jessica knew that her sister had a dentist appointment that day.

There was a shocked silence at the other end of the phone. Slowly, Janet said, "She'll really do it?"

"Sure. I can talk her into anything."

"Wednesday it is, then."

"Great," Jessica said. "Oh, but I won't be there. I've got a dentist appointment on Wednesday." She hung up the phone a moment later, waited, then dialed Janet's number again. The line was busy, just as she thought it would be. Janet was passing the word along. By the end of the evening every Unicorn in Sweet Valley would know that Elizabeth Wakefield *was* going to make Lois Waller eat shaving cream. The plan was going to work!

Nine

◇

Elizabeth's eyes were just fluttering open on Wednesday morning when Jessica put her plan into action. "Lizzie," she said, "you know what you should wear today? Your pink and white striped shirt and your white pants. You always look so good in that outfit."

Elizabeth rubbed her eyes. "OK," she mumbled sleepily. "Maybe I will."

"You'll look great," Jessica said cheerfully.

So far, so good, she thought. This was the day when *it* was going to happen, when Elizabeth Wakefield was going to do her pledge task. Only Elizabeth wasn't going to know a thing about it.

Jessica had set it all up the night before. She almost giggled when she thought about how she had called Lois and asked her to the Dairi Burger.

She had done a perfect Elizabeth imitation. She was only sorry no one had been around to appreciate it.

First she had put on her calmest, friendliest voice. Elizabeth would be nice to a cockroach. "Hi, Lois, this is Elizabeth Wakefield," she'd said.

"Elizabeth!" Lois was thrilled. "Hi, thanks for—I mean, how are you?"

Oh, brother, thought Jessica, but she had been Miss Polite. "Oh, just fine, thank you. Listen, I was wondering if you'd like to get a sundae at the Dairi Burger after school tomorrow." She nearly choked on the words.

"Sure!" Lois exclaimed. "You bet! What time?"

Jessica could barely believe she was actually making a date with Lois Waller, the school hippopotamus. "I'll meet you on the front steps after the last bell. OK?"

"Great! This will be so much fun!"

Fun! Jessica had thought as she hung up. Eating in public with Lois would be about as much fun as having her head shaved. But, she kept reminding herself, it wasn't going to hurt her image. Everyone would think she was Elizabeth, friend to the world.

So that day Jessica put on a purple dress, and Elizabeth wore the outfit Jessica had suggested. Jessica wore her hair down and Elizabeth wore hers pinned back. Elizabeth's face was free of makeup and Jessica carefully put on lip gloss, eye shadow, and mascara. The girls barely looked like twins.

After school Mrs. Wakefield picked Elizabeth up right on schedule and started off for the dentist. Jessica watched from a second-floor window. The minute they were gone she dashed into the girls' room. She changed into her own pink and white striped shirt and white pants. Then she pinned her hair back, removed her plastic bracelets, and washed off the makeup. *There,* she said to herself. *Just like Elizabeth.*

Casually, Jessica walked into the hall and through the corridors to the front steps. Lois was already there.

"Hi, Elizabeth," said Lois, awkwardly clambering off the wall she'd been sitting on. "Thanks again for asking me. It's so nice to do things with a friend."

Jessica cringed. Her pal, the blimp. "Hi, Lois," she said with Elizabeth's nicest, friendliest smile. Then her mind went blank. What would Elizabeth do? What would she say? "How's history going?"

"History," Lois scoffed. She started talking and didn't stop until they reached the Dairi Burger.

Inside, Jessica glanced around and saw Janet, Betsy, Kimberly, and Lila sitting near an empty table. As soon as the Unicorns saw Lois, they began to turn red from trying not to laugh. Jessica quickly walked up to the counter, where she and Lois ordered hot fudge sundaes.

"With marshmallow creme," Lois added. "And nuts. And cherry syrup. Oh, and toasted coconut."

Jessica nearly gagged at Lois's order, but she kept an angelic expression on her face.

"That'll be about five minutes," said the man behind the counter.

"Let's go find a table," Jessica suggested.

She steered Lois to an empty one near the Unicorns.

While they waited for their order, Jessica tried to concentrate on acting like Elizabeth. Every once in a while she thought Lois looked at her strangely. *Remember*, she kept telling herself, *you're quiet, calm, sincere, nice. You like school. You like math. You like* Lois. She was starting to worry.

Just then their order was called out. Jessica jumped up and looked around. "Gee, it's really crowded today," she said. "Why don't you hold our table? I'll go get the sundaes."

"OK," said Lois.

Jessica saw Lila grinning at the next table. Then Betsy stood up and followed at a safe distance. Just as Jessica put the sundaes on a tray, Betsy took her by the elbow and pulled her behind a column. She was holding a spoon and a can of shaving cream.

Jessica crouched down low and balanced the tray on her knees. She took the spoon from Betsy, scraped the whipped cream off Lois's sundae, and dumped it into a nearby trash can. Then she shook the can of shaving cream and squirted a huge amount on the sundae, making peaks and swirls. Betsy disappeared, and Jessica casually walked to her table.

"Here we go," she said brightly as she sat down. She set Lois's sundae in front of her.

Lois stared at it. Then she looked up at Jessica. "Hey," she said. She was frowning.

Jessica nearly fainted. Had Lois figured everything out? "What? What's wrong?" she asked nervously.

"They forgot the coconut."

Jessica trembled with relief. "It's probably underneath," she said shakily. She scooped the cherry off the top of her sundae and held it in front of her. "Cheers," she said.

Lois smiled happily. She took an enormous spoonful of cream, toasted Jessica's raised spoon with it, and aimed it toward her mouth, her eyes closed in anticipation.

"Ew, ew! Ick! Yuck!" Lois spat the shaving cream into her napkin. "What is this? This isn't—" Lois stopped. At the next table Lila, Betsy, Kimberly, and Janet were laughing hysterically. Across from her, the girl she thought was Elizabeth was covering her mouth with a napkin and giggling.

"It's a joke!" Jessica cried, when she was able to talk again. "It's shaving cream!"

Lois's lips began to quiver. "Elizabeth, how

could you do this to me?" Her voice dropped to a whisper as her eyes filled with tears. "You were always nice to me. Now you're acting just like Jessica. I—I don't understand." Very slowly, she stood up. Then she walked out of the Dairi Burger, crying silently. She didn't look back.

Janet sat across from Jessica. "Well, you did it." She sounded surprised. "I have to admit, I didn't think you would, but you did. We'll let you know soon about the club."

The only way to prevent the Unicorns from finding out the truth would be to keep Elizabeth from discovering what she had done. So that night Jessica called Janet, proposing that the Unicorns not congratulate Elizabeth on her pledge task until they were sure that they wanted her in the club. "You know how hurt Elizabeth would be if you rejected her after all that she's gone through," Jessica was explaining to Janet with a sympathetic tone.

Now Jessica was temporarily off the hook! At least until their first meeting. By then she was sure that she'd be able to handle her sister.

The next day Jessica went to her ballet lesson feeling great. If she could fool Elizabeth, Lois, and all the Unicorns, how hard could it be to get Madame André to see the truth—that Jessica Wakefield was a terrific dancer.

It didn't work out that way.

Jessica was dressed in regulation pink and

black. Her hair was in a neat braid. She was dancing really well. But, still, Madame André never
had anything nice to say to her. Toward the end of
class Jessica did a jeté that she knew was much
better than anyone else's. Madame André looked
right at her and said coolly, "Next time, back
straighter." That did it.

In the changing room Jessica yanked off her
ballet slippers, pulled a skirt over her leotard, and
stomped out.

Elizabeth gathered up her things and ran after
her. "Hey, Jessica! What's the matter? Wait!"

Jessica was outside by the time Elizabeth
caught up with her. "That does it! I quit."

"You what?" Elizabeth cried. "Don't quit!
Please. This is the only thing left that we do together."

"Don't worry about that. You're getting into
the Unicorn Club."

"What are you talking about?"

Oops! How had she let that slip? Jessica had
to think. "I have a feeling they'll change their
minds. Because of me, I mean."

"Thanks, Jess, but I really doubt it. Anyway, I
still don't think you should quit ballet."

Jessica was feeling a little calmer. "Neither do
I, but Madame André is totally unfair. She hates
me. Why should I be tortured twice a week?"

"So you're just going to let her get the better
of you? Why don't you stand up to her? Get back
at her."

"Yeah, I guess staying in class would really teach her," Jessica said sarcastically.

"Oh, you know what I mean," Elizabeth said lightly. "Besides, it's not like you to give up."

"I'm not giving up."

"Aren't you? This is the only ballet class in Sweet Valley. Once we stop dancing in gym, ballet will be over for you. You're letting Madame André keep you from something you love."

Jessica knew that was true.

"Why don't you try one more class?"

"Maybe," Jessica said reluctantly.

"Jessica, please." Elizabeth's voice rose slightly.

"OK, OK, OK. One more chance for Madame Keep-Your-Back-Straight, and that's it."

Jessica showed up for ballet on Tuesday almost sure it would be her last class. But something happened that changed her mind.

Just before the lesson ended, Madame André called the girls around her and said, "I have a very important announcement. In two months all of you will perform for the public." There was an excited murmur from the girls until Madame held up her hand. "The Dance Studio will hold a recital at the high school auditorium, and all of Sweet Valley will be there." Madame's eyes gleamed with excitement. "I have many times danced on the stage, and no experience can match it. This class will perform a lovely scene from the ballet *Coppélia*. Do you know the story?"

The girls shook their heads.

"*Alors*, I will tell you then," said Madame André. "*Coppélia* is the story of Swanilda, a beautiful girl who is in love with a handsome man named Franz. Swanilda is afraid that Franz loves Coppélia, a girl he has seen from afar in an old doll shop. Then she learns that Coppélia is only a doll and her dream of marrying Franz comes true. But before that, Swanilda and her friends dance in the shop with the lovely mechanical dolls, and this is the scene we will do. It has many charming parts. Then, of course, we need Swanilda herself. Her solo is very beautiful, but very difficult. A very good dancer is needed for that part.

"I suggest you all practice hard. Soon I will hold auditions for the recital, and each of you will have your chance. Are there any questions?"

"What does Swanilda wear?" asked Jessica, thinking of filmy white gowns and silver crowns.

"Not purple sashes," snapped the teacher.

For heaven's sake, wouldn't she ever forget that? So she had gotten off on the wrong foot, thought Jessica. There was still such a thing as forgiving and forgetting.

Right then and there Jessica promised herself to stick with Madame André's class no matter what. She would practice hard. She would make Madame André see how good she was, and she would win the part of Swanilda. When the Dance Studio held its recital, Jessica Wakefield would be the star.

Ten

◇

That evening Jessica burst into the kitchen screaming Elizabeth's name. "You're in the Unicorn Club! Lila just called. They held a special meeting to vote on you."

Elizabeth just stood there, absolutely amazed. Then she threw her arms around her sister. "Oh, Jess, that's wonderful! But what made them change their minds? I mean, how did I get in?"

Jessica was ready for this. "I told you. Because you're *my* sister. They want to keep me happy."

"You just joined and they did this for you? They must be crazy about you."

"They do like me an awful lot," Jessica said modestly.

"I'm so glad they decided against that awful pledge task," Elizabeth went on. "They must have

realized how much it would have hurt Lois's feelings. You know, Lois has been out of school for
four days. She must be really sick or something."

"Must be," Jessica said. She was feeling a little
nervous about Lois. Suppose shaving cream was
poison after all? *Oh, don't be silly*, she told herself.
Lois's parents probably just got tired of looking at
her and sent her off to a fat farm. That was much
more likely. Anyhow, the Unicorn Club was the
important thing.

"Oh, Lizzie, don't make any plans for tomorrow. Unicorns always hold their meetings on
Wednesdays."

"Great!" Elizabeth said. And she meant it. If
Jessica liked the club so much, it had to be fun.
Besides, the Unicorns must be pretty nice since
they decided she didn't have to play that trick on
Lois. And from now on she'd be with Jessica all
the time!

Jessica looked at Elizabeth's cheerful face and
started congratulating herself all over again. Look
how happy she had made her sister! Of course,
there might be a few bad moments during the
meeting if one of the girls said something about
Elizabeth's pledge task. Jessica put the thought
aside. Probably nobody would. If the subject did
come up, Jessica would change it fast. Anyway,
Elizabeth had nothing to complain about. She
hadn't done anything she didn't want to and she
was *still* in the club. Jessica had done her a big
favor.

The next day Elizabeth was sitting on the floor of Ellen Riteman's bedroom, surrounded by Unicorns. She had been there for forty-five minutes. She knew because she must have looked at her watch about twelve times. Everybody else seemed to be having a great time, but she was bored to death. This just couldn't be what the meetings were really like.

She looked around Ellen's room. She had never seen so many rainbows in her life. They were on the walls, hanging from the ceiling, on her wastebasket. She even had them on her hairbrush and her telephone. Maybe she should count them. That would help her stay awake.

"Attention, please!" Janet called from Ellen's bed. "Did everybody see the new Cole Derek TV movie last night?"

The girls nodded their heads. Well, Elizabeth thought, they were going to discuss the movie. That could be interesting. Jessica had only gotten her to watch part of it, but Elizabeth had read the book.

"Isn't Cole *cute*?" sighed Tamara Chase, one of the eighth graders.

"Just dreamy," Kimberly said with her eyes half-closed.

"I'd do anything to go out with him," Ellen said.

Elizabeth felt as though her head were filling up with oatmeal.

"Did you hear he's going to be in a miniseries

next month for *four* nights, *The Pioneers*, or something," Lila put in.

Elizabeth perked up. "That was a fantastic book!"

The other girls looked at her as though she were speaking Martian.

Jessica quickly changed the subject. "Did you hear what Sandra Ferris wore to the Dairi Burger the other night? A bright red bra under a white blouse! You could see the whole thing!"

"She loves people to stare at her. She's as bad as Jennifer Norris."

Elizabeth felt lost. She had never even heard of these kids they were talking about.

"That reminds me," said Janet, "I found out something we've all been wanting to know for weeks."

Elizabeth straightened up a little.

"I found out what size bra Leslie Carlisle wears."

Lila nearly shrieked. "What? What size?"

Janet paused dramatically. "Are you ready for this? Thirty-six E."

There was a chorus of *wows*, but Elizabeth just stared into space.

"And you know who likes her?" Janet went on.

"Every single boy in school?" asked Jessica.

"Close. Colin Harmon."

"Colin Harmon," cooed Ellen. "He's so cute."

Elizabeth thought, *If I hear "He's so cute" one more time, I think I'll throw up.* She checked her watch again and stifled a yawn.

Jessica poked her. How could her sister be so rude? She had hardly said one word during the whole meeting. How ungrateful! If she kept this up, having her in the club was going to be awful.

"Well," Lila was saying, "I don't know who my idea of a dream date is. Maybe Cole Derek. What about you, Elizabeth?"

"Hmm?" Elizabeth tried to reel her mind in.

"Who would be your dream date?" Lila repeated.

Oh, brother, thought Jessica. This was going to be good. *Please don't say anything too weird*, she silently begged her sister.

"Dream date?" Elizabeth repeated. "Nobody, I guess. I'm not really interested in—"

"In any one person," Jessica finished hastily. "Right, Elizabeth? I mean, there are just so many. Elizabeth likes tons of guys. I'll tell you my dream date. It's Jake Sommers from *Days of Turmoil*."

"Oh, Jake Sommers!" breathed Tamara. "He's so cute."

The meeting dragged on. Centuries seemed to pass before Janet finally announced that the meeting was adjourned. "Let's go to the Dairi Burger," she added.

As the girls stretched and began getting their things together, Ellen came over to Elizabeth. "I heard all about your pledge task!" She grinned.

Jessica turned pale. "Lizzie," she said quickly. "How's the paper going?"

But Ellen was rushing on.

"I just wish I could have been there. I would have loved to see Lois's face when she shoveled in that shaving cream. Listen, are you coming to the Dairi Burger?"

Elizabeth was speechless. "No," she finally said, her mind racing. She knew instantly what must have happened: *Jessica* had done her pledge task. She had lied to her. She had impersonated her. Her own twin had betrayed her. "Jessica," said Elizabeth, her voice shaking with anger, "I will never forgive you for this as long as I live." Elizabeth turned on her heel and walked out.

"Gosh. What's her problem?" said Ellen to Jessica.

"Beats me," Jessica replied uncomfortably. "Come on, let's go."

Elizabeth had never been so angry. She walked into the house and slammed the kitchen door behind her.

"What are you doing here?" she cried when she saw her mother.

"I finished up early." Mrs. Wakefield stood back to get a good look at Elizabeth. "How are you?"

"Not so wonderful." Elizabeth sighed.

"Sit here and talk to me while I start dinner."

"Well," Elizabeth said slowly, "Jessica got me into the Unicorn Club."

"You don't look very happy about it."

"I went to my first meeting and it was horrible. It was boring, and I didn't pay attention, and they asked me a question, and I said something really stupid. But Mom, the worst thing is that they don't *do* anything. They just sit around and gossip. I hated the meeting." Of course, she wasn't going to tell her mother what really happened at the meeting.

Mrs. Wakefield left the potatoes she was peeling and sat down next to her daughter. "Honey, I'm not surprised."

"I had a feeling you wouldn't be. You said the club didn't sound right for me. I didn't want to listen."

"What I really meant was that you and Jessica may look alike, but you are two very different people."

"I guess the club shows how different we are," Elizabeth said thoughtfully. "But Mom, I still feel like I'm losing Jessica."

"Oh, honey," said Mrs. Wakefield, "you may not spend as much time with Jessica as you used to, but you'll never lose her. She's your identical twin. Do you know how special that is?"

Elizabeth started to smile. "Yeah."

"But even if you are a twin, you're also *you*. I think it's time for you to stop following Jessica, even if it's hard at first. Do what *you* want to do.

Try being on your own. After a while I think you're going to like it."

On my own, thought Elizabeth. Well, she already had Amy and Julie and *The Sweet Valley Sixers.* Maybe she was starting to be on her own after all.

And as Elizabeth-on-her-own, there were a few things she had to straighten out.

Eleven

◇

Elizabeth headed straight for the phone in her parents' bedroom. She was going to call Lois Waller right away, before another minute went by.

A woman answered the phone.

Elizabeth cleared her throat. "Is Lois there, please?"

"Who's calling?"

"It's . . . Elizabeth Wakefield."

There was silence on the other end of the line. "I'm not sure she'll want to talk to you. Hold on."

Elizabeth heard muffled voices and several bumps, as if the phone were being passed back and forth. Finally Lois's voice came through the receiver. "Elizabeth?"

"Lois, I'm calling to explain and apologize—"

"Why did you do it? The other girls used to tease me, but never you."

"Look, it wasn't me," she said. "You know I wouldn't do something like that."

"Oh, come on. I'm not blind."

"Look, it was Jessica. It's a long story, but she was tricking those other girls into thinking she was me. Lois, I'm really sorry. I feel terrible."

"I'm glad it wasn't you." Some of the tension had left Lois's voice. Then she added, "Everyone was laughing at me. I thought I'd die."

"I know. It's the meanest thing I've ever heard of. I really hope you come back to school soon."

"I can't go back." Lois suddenly sounded tearful. "Not after that. It was too humiliating. We can't afford it, but my mom's looking into private schools."

"Oh, come back, Lois, please," pleaded Elizabeth. "You'll find kids like Jessica and Janet at any school. Why don't you sit with Amy and Julie and me at lunch tomorrow? We're starting a newspaper. Maybe you'll have some ideas."

"Well . . ." Lois said slowly. "Maybe. Thanks for calling, Elizabeth. I feel much better."

"I'll look for you tomorrow." As Elizabeth hung up, she heard Jessica rummaging around in their bedroom. She marched right in.

Jessica sighed when she saw her. "Now, Lizzie, don't—"

Elizabeth cut her off. "For once, Jessica Wakefield, you are going to listen to me. First of all, I want to say that I have never been so mad at anyone in my entire life. And you know what makes me maddest of all? Not what you did to Lois, even though it was awful. And not that you lied to me about how I got into the club."

"But what, then?"

"That you thought it was perfectly fine to pretend you were me and let everyone think *I* would do such a thing. You acted as though I just don't count for anything."

"But you know I don't feel that way!" Jessica protested.

"Then you'd better start acting like it. I told Lois that I wasn't the one who did it. I want *you* to apologize to her."

"No way!" exclaimed Jessica.

Elizabeth decided it was time she used Jessica's tactics on Jessica. "I'm quitting the Unicorn Club, by the way."

Jessica didn't try to keep the relief out of her voice. "Well, I didn't think the club was exactly right for you."

"That is, I'm quitting if you apologize to Lois."

"I told you—" Jessica sounded very annoyed.

"If you don't do it, I might just stay in. And as a loyal Unicorn, I'll have to tell Lila and Janet and all the Unicorns everything—and I mean *everything!*"

"This is blackmail!" Jessica shrieked.

"You should really apologize in person," Elizabeth went on, as though Jessica hadn't said a thing.

"I won't!"

"Mom might be interested in all this, too."

"*All right*. I'll do it. Are you satisfied?"

"Yes. Thank you. You've got exactly a week to apologize." Elizabeth turned to her homework without saying another word.

Exactly one week later Elizabeth sat with Lois Waller on the wall by the front steps of Sweet Valley Middle School.

"I can't believe how much everyone liked the paper," Elizabeth exclaimed happily. "I have only two copies left—one for me, and one for my parents."

"Hey, Elizabeth, *The Sweet Valley Sixers* is great!" Lila Fowler came down the steps carrying her book bag and a copy of the paper. "I really liked Caroline's gossip column. How does she find out all that stuff?"

"I'm not sure," Elizabeth said with a smile, "but I'm glad you liked it."

"The other Unicorns liked the paper, too. When's the next one coming out?"

"In a couple of weeks, I hope."

"Great! See you!" Lila ran across the lawn to Ellen Riteman, then turned around and yelled, "Hey, Lois, are you working on the paper, too?"

"Not yet," Lois answered.

"Why not? You could do a diet column and call it 'Advice from Miss Piggy'!"

Lila and Ellen burst out laughing and walked on.

"Jerks," Lois said. "I *hate* them."

"They're not my favorite people. Someone should give them a taste of their own medicine sometime," Elizabeth thought aloud.

"Hey," said Lois, "how come you asked me to meet you here anyway?"

"You'll see," replied Elizabeth.

Just then Jessica appeared at the door and walked slowly down the steps. "Hi, Lois," she said uncomfortably.

Lois stared down at the ground. "Hi."

"Um, Lois," Jessica began, her face reddening. "I wanted to tell you that I'm sorry about what happened at the Dairi Burger. I guess it was sort of mean."

"It was very mean," Lois said vehemently, jerking her head up to look at Jessica.

"I know I hurt your feelings. So I'm sorry." She paused. "You don't have to forgive me. I just wanted to apologize."

"Thanks, Jessica," Lois said quietly. "I'm glad you did." She looked at Elizabeth. "See you at lunch again tomorrow?"

"Sure. We'll talk more about the paper."

Lois hurried toward the waiting school bus.

"I know you didn't want to do that," Elizabeth said to Jessica, "but it meant a lot to Lois. And to me."

"It's just too bad she can't take a joke."

Elizabeth gave her sister a look. "Anyway, I won't tell her it was a pledge task, and I won't give you away to the Unicorns, if you never ask me to do your homework again."

"All right . . ." Jessica's voice trailed off. A moment later her blue-green eyes were sparkling again. "Hey, I meant to tell you. The paper was great. Everyone was talking about it. Maybe I should work on it."

Elizabeth had to smile. She had been dying for this to happen, and now it didn't seem important. "I wouldn't say no, but are you really, really sure you want to?"

Jessica grinned. "Well, if you put it that way . . . I'm still awfully busy."

Twelve

◇

"For heaven's sake, what is going on here?" Mrs. Wakefield was standing in the doorway to the twins' room. They had been shouting at each other so loudly, neither one had heard her calling. "In exactly five more minutes you two are going to be late for school."

"Mom, Jessica is a pig," Elizabeth snapped.

"Elizabeth! That's a terrible thing to say," exclaimed her mother.

"Well, she *is* a pig. She spilled soda on my desk. And look at her side of the room."

Her mother stared at the litter of clothing, paper, crumbs, and makeup and murmured, "Terrible, but accurate."

"My half wouldn't be so messy if you weren't crowding me out," Jessica told her twin.

"All right! We don't have time to discuss this

now," said Mrs. Wakefield. "We'll talk about it tonight."

Over dessert that evening Mr. Wakefield
grinned at the twins and said, "Get ready, girls.
We have some big news. You're each going to have
your own room."

"Our own rooms!" shrieked both girls simultaneously.

"That's right." Mrs. Wakefield laughed. "I just
never thought about it until this morning. All we
have to do is turn the guest room down the hall
into a bedroom."

"Then I'll never have to live in a messy room
again!" Elizabeth looked ecstatic.

"And I can be just as messy as I like," Jessica
said with a satisfied smile.

"I don't think that's the idea, Jess," Steven
remarked, but he was smiling more cheerfully
than he had for a long time.

"We can redecorate, too," Mrs. Wakefield
went on. "Jessica, you can stick to pink and white
if you want, it's up to you. Elizabeth, you'll probably want something entirely different."

"I want navy blue curtains." Elizabeth was
smiling dreamily. "And plain white walls. And a
gigantic desk. I just can't wait."

"Then," Mr. Wakefield told her, "we'll try to
get it all finished this weekend."

After dinner Jessica and Elizabeth went up to
their room. "Maybe by next week we won't be

roommates anymore," Jessica said. "You know, even after all the fighting we've been doing, I'll kind of miss sharing a room with you."

"You will?"

"Sure. We've shared a room all our lives. I'll miss lying in bed at night talking."

"Me, too." Elizabeth sighed.

"But," Jessica added, "I won't miss your ten million books."

"And I won't miss your piles of clothes."

"Or all your lectures on neatness."

"Or your candy wrappers in my bed and the crumbs on . . ." Elizabeth grinned. "We'd better cut this out before we start fighting again."

"I know!" Jessica leaped up from her bed. "Let's go practice ballet. The auditions are coming up really soon."

"I don't think I will." Elizabeth looked toward her night table. "I've got a new book of poems I want to read."

"You can read that any old time!"

Elizabeth smiled at her sister. "I want to tell you something. A couple of weeks ago I would have said yes even though I didn't feel like practicing, which I don't, just so we would be together. But now I don't have to stick to you like glue. I can do what I really want to."

Jessica looked astounded. "You mean you didn't before? I sure always did what I wanted!"

"Well, that was the trouble. So did I—always do what you wanted, I mean. But not anymore."

Jessica raised an eyebrow. "I'm not sure I'm going to like this," she said. But her aqua-blue eyes were twinkling. If she really tried, Jessica was sure she would still be able to get her way with Elizabeth. Right now it wasn't important, so she headed for the door. "See you later, big sister."

As Jessica left the room, Elizabeth gave a contented sigh, settled back on her bed, and picked up her book.

The Wakefields spent the entire weekend fixing up the twins' rooms. Everyone pitched in. On Sunday Steven and the girls were painting the guest room off-white for Elizabeth. Steven kept humming and sloshing paint on the wall in time to a tape on his Walkman.

"You've been in a good mood lately," Jessica remarked.

Steven winked at her. "Really?"

"Yeah, lost your fangs and everything. So what was going on with you? Is it safe to ask now?"

"Sure. It just took me a while to get over Roberta dumping me."

Elizabeth stopped painting. "Roberta dumped you?"

"Why?" Jessica gasped. "Because you're older?"

"Well," Steven said, looking uncomfortable, "not exactly."

"Why, then? Come on, tell," Jessica coaxed.

"OK, it doesn't really bother me anymore. But I don't want you kidding me about it and don't spread it around." He grinned sheepishly. "She said I was too immature."

"Oh, no!" Jessica shrieked, and started to giggle.

"What does she want? An old man?" Elizabeth cried.

"I think she has a crush on some college kid—not that he's interested in her," Steven said. "It was pretty hard to take, especially with the high school kids saying I was a nerd for dating a baby. Anyhow, it's fine now." Steven cleared his throat. "See, there's this other girl—a sophomore—"

"Oh, an older woman!" squealed Jessica. "That'll show Roberta."

"And this sophomore doesn't think you're so immature?" Elizabeth smiled.

"Oh, no. Not Mandy," Steven answered. He raised his eyebrows. "We sit next to each other in biology. We're going to dissect a carp together."

Jessica wrinkled her nose. "How romantic," she said. She had started painting again.

"You know," Elizabeth said thoughtfully, "maybe Roberta didn't really mean what she said. Maybe she was just upset for getting grounded and kicked out of the Unicorns and all."

"What do you mean kicked out?" Steven asked. "She dropped out."

Jessica nearly dropped her paintbrush.

"She got really annoyed after Janet Howell

asked me to go to a party with her," Steven went on. "And she quit."

Jessica's mouth dropped open, and Elizabeth started to laugh.

"Then—then," Jessica gasped, "here I was keeping it quiet and Janet knew all along you were the boy Roberta was seeing. She never said a word to me about you."

"What could she say? I just told her to wait and look me up when she gets to high school. I'm not going to make a hobby of dating eighth-grade girls.

Jessica eyed Steven with new respect. "So the Unicorns—the most outstanding girls in school— were practically fighting over my brother!"

"Yep." Steven bowed. "Those Unicorns have great taste in men."

"Maybe so, but they're not very nice." Elizabeth couldn't resist bringing this up. "I mean, picking on Lois Waller . . . how mean can you get? I wonder how they would like it if everyone laughed at *them*."

Jessica raised her eyebrows. "It's silly even to talk about. That could just *never* happen."

"Well, somebody should show them—" Elizabeth stopped speaking as, in a flash, it came to her. A brilliant idea. She turned her head away from Jessica and tried to smother the laugh that was bubbling up. Somebody *would* show them. Elizabeth Wakefield!

Thirteen

◇

The first chance she had, Elizabeth slipped into her parents' bedroom and shut the door. Then she dialed Lois Waller's number.

"Lois," she said softly, "how would you like to play a trick on the Unicorns?"

"I'm dying to get back at them. What do you have in mind?"

"I have a great idea. Listen to this. Tomorrow afternoon you and Amy and I follow the Unicorns to the Dairi Burger. You act like you're by yourself, while Amy and I get a table near the Unicorns. Then you go over and really make up to them, like you're sorry you got upset about the trick they played."

Elizabeth lowered her voice to a whisper and told Lois the rest of her plan. "So what do you think?" she said when she was done.

"Neato! If it works, I'll be so happy I'll—I'll go on a diet! I think you're a *genius!*"

The next afternoon Elizabeth and Amy sauntered into the Dairi Burger, with Lois a few steps behind. "Over there," Elizabeth muttered to Lois. Six members of the Unicorn Club—Jessica, Janet, Lila, Ellen, Betsy, and Kimberly—were already sitting at a booth waiting for their order.

Lois walked over to the candy machine, Elizabeth sat down, and Amy put their order in. Elizabeth saw Lila whisper something to Ellen and point to Lois. Knowing Lila, it was something really mean, thought Elizabeth.

Elizabeth glanced at Lois, who still seemed to be poring over the candy selection, and gave her the thumbs-up sign.

Lois acted as if she had just spotted the Unicorns. "Hi! Gee, I wanted you guys to know I've been thinking it over and that trick you played on me was really pretty funny. I mean, I know the Unicorns like girls to be good sports and all. . . ."

Lila rolled her eyes. "Oh, you're such a good sport, maybe we should consider you for membership?"

As the other girls started to snicker, Order Eighteen was called out.

Lila stood up.

"Oh, I'll get your order!" Lois gushed. "You don't have to do that."

Lila smirked at the rest of the girls. "Oh, hey, sure, Lois. Why not?"

"Number eighteen!" the man at the counter called again.

"That's us, Lois. You'd better hurry," Lila said.

"You're on!" Elizabeth whispered to Amy. Then she got up and followed Lois.

Amy pulled a camera out of her tote bag and headed for the Unicorn table.

"How about a picture for *The Sweet Valley Sixers*?" she asked. All the girls at the table turned on dazzling smiles just as though Amy had turned on a switch. "Beautiful! Just a couple more," she cried.

While Amy was flashing away, Elizabeth pulled Lois, tray and all, behind a column.

"Three shakes, two hot fudge sundaes, and Lila's strawberry sundae with chocolate ice cream," Lois reported.

"Go ahead." Elizabeth grinned. She held the tray while Lois spooned whipped cream off Lila's sundae and piled it high with shaving cream. "Now let me get back to our booth before you take the tray to the girls." Elizabeth hid the can of shaving cream in her book bag. Then she went back to the booth and waited while Lois stood at Jessica's table, passing out the shakes and sundaes. When Lois had served everyone, Elizabeth strolled over to the Unicorns. "Hi, guys," she said.

"Lizzie!" Jessica squealed. She sounded more embarrassed than glad.

"Hi," muttered Janet.

Lila dipped her spoon into her sundae and raised it to her mouth.

"Hey!" Elizabeth cried. "I wouldn't, you guys. I think that . . . *she*"—Elizabeth nodded toward Lois, who was returning the tray—"might try to get back at you."

"Oh, come on, Elizabeth," said Lila. "Lois wouldn't have the nerve to do anything like that to one of *us*."

"I don't know," Elizabeth replied slowly. "I wouldn't let her get *my* sundae."

"Well, I'm not worried," said Jessica. She put a mouthful of whipped cream on her spoon and tasted it. "See? It's fine."

"So's mine," said Ellen, licking her lips.

"And mine," said Kimberly.

"And mine," said Janet and Betsy.

"And m—" Lila started to say, but choked and spat out a mouthful of shaving cream. She stood up, gasping and gagging. Her eyes were closed, her face was screwed up, and her tongue was sticking out. "Oh! That is *foul*! Get me water. Who's got water? Anything!" She grabbed Ellen's vanilla shake and took a long swallow.

"Don't get any shaving cream in it!" Ellen cried.

"Oh, shut up!"

Lila suddenly noticed Amy had appeared with her camera and was clicking away.

"Stop that!" she shrieked.

Everyone in the Dairi Burger was roaring with laughter, even the men behind the counter. Elizabeth and Amy giggled so hard, they couldn't talk. The only ones not laughing were the girls in the Unicorn Club. Lila was a brilliant shade of red.

Elizabeth tried to get herself under control, but she and Amy and Lois were practically falling over.

"I can't believe it!" exclaimed Janet.

"This has never happened to the Unicorns," wailed Kimberly. "She made us look like fools."

"Come on, let's go." Janet stood up. She headed for the door, with the other Unicorns straggling along behind her.

"Good riddance!" Lois called to them gaily.

The Unicorns ignored her as they rushed to the door.

Lois turned back to Elizabeth. "I did it! I really did it!" she cried. "I made fools of the Unicorns! Lois Waller strikes back!"

Fourteen

◇

One afternoon, two weeks later, Elizabeth was lying on her bed admiring her new room. It felt good just to be there. She had picked out a cream-colored carpet to go with the off-white walls, her curtains were a navy print with yellow trim, and she probably had the biggest desk in Sweet Valley.

There was a knock on the door and Steven poked his head in. "Hey, why's the door shut?"

"I'm just enjoying my room." Elizabeth smiled. "Have you and Mandy dissected the carp yet?"

"Yeah, yesterday. It was wonderful. My hand brushed Mandy's as we both reached for the same scalpel. Then our eyes met over the—"

"Stop!" shrieked Elizabeth. "I don't want to know what your eyes met over. I'm sure it was gross."

"Wait until tomorrow." Steven put his hand over his heart. "We dissect a sheep's eye."

"Some romance." Elizabeth laughed. "But everything's going well for you, isn't it?"

Steven nodded cheerfully.

"For me, too. The Unicorns never figured out that the trick we played on Lila was really my idea. They were so relieved I didn't run those pictures in the *Sixers*—which I never meant to do—they just stopped mentioning the whole thing. It's lucky Caroline Pearce didn't find out about it or—oh, gosh, it's almost time to leave for ballet. I'd better get Jess."

Steven waved and she hurried downstairs. A few minutes later she and Jessica were headed toward the Dance Studio.

"Should we take the shortcut?" Elizabeth asked.

"And go by the Mercandy house? No way. Everybody says Mrs. Mercandy's a witch and the place is haunted."

"The place is creepy, but she can't be a *witch*." Elizabeth glanced at her watch. "I guess we have enough time to go the regular way. I just don't want to be late."

"*You* don't want to. Imagine how I feel! I'm trying to get Madame André to like me."

Someone whizzed by on a bicycle. "Hi, Jessica!" called a male voice.

"That was Bruce Patman!" exclaimed Jessica.

"Nice of him to say hi to *me*," muttered Elizabeth.

"Oh, come on. He doesn't know you. Besides, did you notice what he called me?"

"Yeah, your name."

"Exactly. No more 'blondie.' Everybody's starting to see we really are two different people. We're the new Jessica Wakefield and the new Elizabeth Wakefield."

"That's right. The old Jessica was *never* interested in boys!"

"But the old Elizabeth would never have pulled a trick like the one you pulled on Lila." Jessica smiled slightly. "I was really mad when you told me you thought that up. I felt so humiliated when everyone in the Dairi Burger laughed at us."

"About the same way Lois felt when everybody laughed at her?"

Jessica made a face. "OK. Anyway, you may be a goody-goody, but underneath it all, you're OK."

"Thanks a lot! I guess that's supposed to be a compliment."

Jessica laughed. "What I mean is maybe we don't agree on a lot of things, but you're still my best friend."

"And you're mine!" Elizabeth was really glad Jessica had come right out and said it.

When the twins reached the Dance Studio,

Elizabeth was surprised to see Amy Sutton standing glumly by her mother at the reception desk. "What are you doing here?" she asked.

Amy sighed. "My mother's going through with it. She's actually signing me up for ballet."

"Come on, sweetheart," her mother said, smoothing back Amy's hair. "You'll love it."

"Wanna bet?" muttered Amy.

Elizabeth left her looking as though she were going to be executed.

"*Jetez! Jetez!* Jump! Good, class! Elizabeth, very nice. Jessica, keep your back straight. And one, two, three, four. Good, class, stop."

Jessica leaned over to catch her breath. Madame André had given them a real workout.

"*Alors,*" said Madame. "The auditions are close now. You must be in very good shape for them. And remember that you must work very hard to earn the part of Swanilda. *Comprenez?* Do you understand?" She smiled at Elizabeth.

Jessica's stomach turned to ice. What good was it to be the best dancer in the class if Madame André never noticed?

"*Bien.* Class is dismissed," said the teacher.

The girls hurried to the changing room, but Jessica stood where she was, unable to move. She was beyond thinking about giving up ballet. She had made up her mind. She just *had* to dance the part of Swanilda, no matter what. But what could she do to make it happen?

Will Jessica star in the dance recital? Find out in **Teacher's Pet,** *book two in the Sweet Valley Twins series.*

☐ THE SARA SUMMER   15481/$2.50
by Mary Downing Hahn

Twelve-year-old Emily Sherwood has grown like a beanstalk and all the kids are calling her "Giraffe." What's worse, her best friend has deserted her. Things seem pretty bad until Sara, a tall, tough, wacky and wise New Yorker teaches Emily a thing or two about life.

☐ YOU'RE GOING OUT THERE A   15272/$2.25
KID, BUT YOU'RE COMING BACK A STAR
by Linda Hirsch

Margaret Dapple is ten years old and tired of waiting around to grow up, tired of waiting for everyone—especially her parents and big sister Barbara—to recognize that she is not a baby anymore. So Margaret decides to show them all—she's going to improve her image.

☐ NOW IS NOT TOO LATE   15334/$2.50
by Isabelle Holland

When Cathy arrives on the island to spend the summer with her grandmother, her summer friends warn her to stay away from the Wicked Witch, who turns out to be hauntingly familiar and not a witch at all.

☐ THE SISTERS IMPOSSIBLE   26013/$2.50
by J. D. Landis

As sisters go, Saundra and Lily have never been the best of friends. But the real trouble starts when their father buys younger sister Lily a pair of dancing shoes so she can to go to ballet school with the beautiful and accomplished Saundra.

☐ ANASTASIA KRUPNIK   15338/$2.50
by Lois Lowry

To Anastasia Krupnik, being ten is very confusing. On top of everything her parents are going to have a baby—at their age! It's enough to make a kid want to do something terrible . . .